FROM THE
WINDOW OF
GELATO

FROM THE
WINDOW OF
GELATO

Jaideep Singh Chadha

PARTRIDGE
A Penguin Random House Company

The author can be reached at jaichadha2007@gmail.com

To order additional copies of this book, contact
Partridge India
000 800 10062 62
www.partridgepublishing.com/india
orders.india@partridgepublishing.com

ACKNOWLEDGEMENTS

I have to admit that this book had very humble beginnings. It was an idea floated by friends which quickly germinated and then blossomed into a flower. Suggestions came in droves as time cantered and now you have the final product in your hands.

The editing was done by my daughter, Mrs Guneet Kaur Bhatti. Thank you Guneet! All your suggestions were very apt and helpful and have been incorporated fully.

I am grateful to Sardar Harbans Singh Noor, the famous Sikh historian from Baltimore, USA, for reading every chapter as it was sent to him through the internet. His suggestions were valuable. Thank you, Veerji, for everything.

I am grateful for the friendship of Gullu Sundar Singh and his sister Priya Rajvansh. I am sorry that they departed so early in life. May their souls rest in peace! I shall always cherish my association with them. Thank you Ms.Ruby Bedi, where ever you are.

It is obvious that without Mr.Tejbans Singh Jauhar, Mr Vikramjit Singh, Ms Anne Cherian, Ms. Jaspreet Nijjer, Mr Vidhu Verma, Mrs Theresa Michaels, Mr. Ajit Singh Walia and Mr. Inderpreet Singh (I.P.), this book would have been a non starter. The photographs on the cover and back are by Mr. Tejbans Singh Jauhar. Many thanks to him. The picture on the back cover was taken on a day when I was in great pain because of a bad fall. It doesn't show, does it? This proves how good a photographer he is! (or, is it due to my ability as an actor?). Thanks are also due to Mr Dharam Vir for designing the cover of the book.

My gratitude goes out to Mrs Navdeep kaur for her inputs. I am grateful to Mr. Tarun Thakur and Ms Tanuja Rana for their patient help because I got stuck repeatedly with my limited computer knowledge.

And then, last but not the least, there is Mrs Gurminder Kaur, my wife.

THIS BOOK IS DEDICATED TO THE LATEST ADDITION IN OUR FAMILY,

SARDAR SABEER SINGH CHADHA, BORN ON THE 18th OF JULY 2013.

OTHER BOOKS BY THE AUTHOR:

THE OTHER SIDE OF GOLF

VINCULUM

MARRIAGE ROCKS

THE FUNNY SIDE OF GOLF

PLEASE MOM! IT'S MY LIFE!

WHY ARE WE STILL LIKE THIS ONLY?

ABOUT THE AUTHOR

Jaideep Singh Chadha was born on the 11 Oct 1949, in Mumbai, India, into an Armed forces family. His early days and education were nomadic because of the regular transfers that his father, Late Iqbal Singh Chadha, had to go through.

He graduated from Indira Gandhi Medical College, Shimla in 1972. He then went on to do Post Graduation in Internal Medicine from the Post Graduate Institute of Medical Research and Education, Chandigarh in 1978.

His writing career began with the publication of his first novel VINCULUM in 1991, following which he has authored six other books. PLEASE MOM! IT'S MY LIFE has been translated into Spanish and Marathi, and is into its' 8th revised edition.

He practices Medicine in Chandigarh. He is a keen golfer. He is also the Founding Member and Ex-President of Toastmasters Club International of Chandigarh.

He is married to Gurminder Kaur Chadha. They have two children, Mrs Guneet Kaur Bhatti and Captain Aman deep Singh Chadha (Merchant Navy). The two went on to contribute 4 children, Shiv Raj Singh, Kabir Singh, Mehar Kaur and Sabir Singh, into the family kitty.

He is a recipient of the Vijay Rattan Award.

PROLOGUE

Society is woven by strands of people who inhabit it, the culture of the region, the traditions formed over the years and by its politics. But all these would collectively fail to hold it together if there were no stories to bind them. It is these stories that have been passed over the years to generations which do that. Not all of them were products of human fantasy and imagination. Most of them were real; they actually happened. These were stories that people related down generations, sitting around a bonfire, sipping rum, toddy, or whatever else they liked to drink.

That is why I wrote these stories about real people, whom I met in the Gelato ice cream parlor of sector 8 in Chandigarh, considered an otherwise sleepy town of the North of India. These will no doubt be talked about as stories from Chandigarh. Maybe, some other writers will be provoked to write more stories of the region that they live in.

These stories originate from a coffee-cum Ice cream parlor, known as the Gelato Ice cream parlor. The value of the parlor is enhanced by the total absence of European styled boulevards in the city where one could enjoy the ample sunshine and whatever the establishments have to offer. It is run by Mrs Monica Sood, who also owns the neighboring bakery, Monica's Puddings and Pies. The two establishments are separated by a passageway. One wall of the ice cream parlor which faces the passageway and the corridor is glass. It offers an excellent view to the happenings on the outside. It is a small booth with dimensions of 12 feet by 16 feet. The owner has placed three tables with three chairs each for those who would like to sit and have their ice creams, cup cakes or coffee. The tables have quaint lace table cloths and a small artificial potted plant in a small plastic pot. Come New Year and Christmas, paper cut outs of bells, bells made out of glass and plastic sprout like mushrooms only to disappear when the festival is over. The interior is very tastefully decorated with the ice cream and cake refrigerators hogging bulk of the area. A small kitchenette and a microwave are neatly hidden behind the serving counter.

We have a table almost dedicated to us. My friends are magnanimous enough to give me the seat which affords a clear view of the outside. From this vantage situation, I can observe the finer nuances of what is happening in the world.

There is a Peepal tree just outside the joint. For many years, it stood unsolicited, like an orphan no one really wanted. Recently, the administration has built a cemented sitting area around it. Hence the contact with civilization has gone up. When the weather is friendly, young couples, and groups of revelers bring their ice creams and other take-aways and sit around the tree. For many reasons, the Peepal tree has been granted a venerated status in Indian mythology. Thus the tree continues to stand there proudly, despite the muck it generates with its' leaves scattering all over and the small fruit which falls on the hapless cars parked under it.

One wonders if it is all bird droppings and not the trees' squashed fruit?

I have been observing all, the thin and the obese who come for bakery products and ice cream. Eating, for the thin is just a need to be fulfilled, most of the times, whereas, just the thought of those goodies give the obese so much pleasure. That is why the expressions differ. The obese go about the business of getting out of their cars, walking slowly to the door of the bakery (they can't walk faster in any case), fantasizing about what they are going to gobble and disappearing into the bakery, a very conscious act, their expression saying it all for anticipated ecstasy. No wonder the real fat ones never think about visiting the dietician. They go to the bakery instead.

The author can be reached at jaichadha2007@gmail.com

THE CAST:

S. P. S. OBEROI: A man of humble origins, he became a multi millionaire in a short span. He is one of the greatest Indian philanthropists known to me personally. He paid 1.2 million dollars as blood money for seventeen Punjabi youths sentenced to death in Dubai for the killing of one Pakistani in a brawl. This is only the tip of the iceberg that S. P. S. Oberoi has done. He continues to perform miracles.

SHAMSHER JANG SINGH PANWAR (SAM): He is a friend I picked up in the Chandigarh Golf Club. He is an extensively travelled, retired corporate honcho. He is as humorous as one can get (also, he has to be funny for he is a Sikh), drinks and eats everything that could come under the category of 'edible'. He has his own story for me to relate.

GULLU: He was an art dealer and critic who lived in the suburbs of London. He was Sam's friend from Bishop Cotton School in Shimla, a hill station located about three hours from Chandigarh. He had a huge house in Sector 5 which prompted him to visit India often. His claim to fame was that he was the brother of acclaimed actress Priya Rajvansh.

PRIYA RAJVANSH: A Shakespearean theatre artist, one of the most beautiful actresses ever to grace the Indian cinema. She was Gullu's sister and became a great friend. It was a tragedy when she was murdered in Mumbai. Hers' is the story I just had to narrate.

RUBY BEDI: A Canada based tantric and spiritualist. I met her through my dear friend Anita Bansal. She was involved with Priya Rajvansh in a very Bollywood—like story.

DARK SAD AND ANGRY SAD: Two young girls I met frequently in the coffee parlor.

THE COFFEE GANG

TEJ BANS JOHAR: An international professional photographer who has travelled extensively. A man possessing a wide spectrum of qualities and a collector of the fine things of life, including the finest alcohol collection which has to be replenished with startling regularity for he has a big heart. He is now into collecting and selling art. A friend, whose knowledge of worldly affairs comes in very handy. His collection also includes high ranking people from nearly all professions. He was instrumental in my meeting Mr S. P. S. Oberoi.

JAGTAR SINGH: My childhood friend. He is also Mr Dependable and a man with a heart of gold. How can destiny play cruel tricks on a man of his credentials, is a mystery to me!

VIKRAMJIT SINGH: A golfer who relocated from Mumbai to Chandigarh and now dabbles in supplying construction material to contractors. He is very heavy on the culinary scene and knows whatever is good in the vegetarian world and its' availability. He is a walking encyclopedia rubbing shoulders with some of the polity and Page 3 people.

VIDHU VERMA: A 23 years old computer engineer, whom I befriended in the Toastmasters Club of Chandigarh, is also my biking partner. We have coffee only on Saturdays and Sundays, for some people also have to work for a living. He is a clone of the Indian cricket opener, Shikar Dhawan and like him, he too is obsessed with his moustache; and of course girls, which would be natural for a normal full bloodied male.

JASPREET NIJJER: Works with the TIMES OF INDIA as a Principal Correspondent. I came to know her when she wrote a piece on one of my books many years ago in her newspaper. She is very fond of coffee, pastries, cakes and loves visiting all the eateries in town, all the while desperately trying to lose weight. The gymnasium is her savior where she regularly works out.

ANNE CHERIAN : The much dimpled lady from the state of Kerala, which is called God's own country because of its bounty. She also works for the TIMES OF INDIA covering schools. She is extremely fond of the Gelato coffee and like Jaspreet, loves to saver goodies in new restaurants of Chandigarh.

JASPREET SINGH PARMAR: An upcoming advocate by profession who is equally fond of coffee. A student of Y. P. S. School, Mohali, he comes with his friends from school some of whom are presently into real estate. We discussed his engagement and subsequent wedding with great anticipation. He is a fast learner and will soon learn the art of being married.

AJIT PAL SINGH WALIA: A young entrepreneur, who was into the book business. I first met him as a patient and then became friends when he started selling my books in schools. He also set up lectures in institutions for me. We made a good team. He would join us for coffee while he was hosting publishers in Chandigarh.

MRS THERESA MICHAELS : Has a Masters degree in Human Resources, she is a cherished friend and advisor. She is the mother of two lovely children, who take part in all activities that their mother is obsessed about. Theresa has since relocated to Mumbai where her activities continue.

CHAPTER 1

It is only in the hill regions would you find two hilly billys, just sitting on their haunches, smoking bidis and sipping hot tea, exchanging gossip and listening to Hindi songs on the transistor, as you pass by, only to find them in the same posture four hours later, as you return. The famous Tibetian Master, Sogyal Rinpoche calls this an Eastern style of *'Active Laziness'*. But in bigger cities, one can't even dream of doing these acts of laziness. Imagine, a New Yorker in a relaxing mode of this kind. Impossible!

Tejbans Jauhar and I, are two 64 year old semi— retired people along with a few others, who can afford to spend quality time doing nothing special, sipping coffee in a coffee parlor in a city like Chandigarh. Not that we don't have worries. We have plenty of those. But for those two hours, between 4 p.m. and 6 p.m., our life moves on a different gear. We just talk about things other than our worries. That is why we consider ourselves the chosen ones, a very rare breed, much to the consternation of passers-by, for one table is always taken. As the clock strikes 4, and more of our kind join in, there is no place left for run-of-the mill coffee drinkers. They would have easily understood, had I placed a placard "WORK IN PROGRESS", for a book was under construction!

As I waited for Tejbans Jauhar (Teji) to arrive, I picked up the edition of *Times Of India* of that day and breezed through it. Suddenly, my eyes latched on to the news item which highlighted the pardon of 17 Punjabi youths by the Government of Dubai who had been sentenced to death by hanging. The newspaper informed me further that a Mr S.P.S.Oberoi had paid 1.2 million dollars in exchange for the lives of the 17 youths from Punjab, whom he did not know from Adam, Tom, Dick or Harry.

I was touched by Mr Oberoi's humanitarian gesture. It was not just a philanthropic gesture. Philanthropy was something that you did out of the generosity of your heart and because you have the money to donate. Here, in the case of Mr Oberoi, it was not just the huge amount of money that he had put in, but also the relentless effort on his part to win a seemingly lost battle. In my book, this transcends philanthropy by a mile and a half.

As I pondered over the issue, Teji walked in. Baloo rang up to find out if I was having coffee. I replied in the affirmative and he too joined us after a short while. Mine wasn't an invitation. The problem with this joint was that people saw us sitting inside and invited themselves in, as if they were walking into our drawing room or that we owned the joint. After having coffee they just thanked us and left, leaving us with the bill. When we started having coffee in Gelato, coffee cost 30 rupees. It was now 63 rupees!

"So what is new?" Baloo asked his usual question. There are people in this world who ask this question without even really wanting to know what is new. It is a matter of habit. But people like me start off narrating what should not be narrated just because someone has asked 'so what else is new!'. That is as foolish a habit as any. I have another friend who asks me the same question a hundred times and I like a fool I tell him a thousand things which I think are new and which I think I should tell him since he has asked me to tell him about 'what is new'. But now, having realized my flawed personality, instead of reeling off my usual habitual dialogues, I asked Baloo, "So what is new with you?"

Without batting an eye, he calmly told me, "Oh! There a hundred things but they can be only told over a few drinks!" That would be neatly tucked away between slip and third man if it was cricket!

"It is the same old thing. Nothing new happened since we met last." I asked him again, "What is new at your end?" He deflected it again like a seasoned politician. I realized there is a certain amount of irritation in my voice.

"What? No rumor? No gossip?"

"Despite the fact that I am the president of the gossip club, I must tell you this story about Socrates, the philosopher. A guy goes to Socrates and says, "Hey Babe! I must tell you about this fellow!"

Socrates replies, "Before you tell me whatever you want to tell me, I would like to know if the information will it be of any use to me?"

The informer replies, "No."

Socrates again asks, "Will it be of any use to you?"

"No." comes the reply.

"Will it help anyone else in society?"

"No." comes the reply again.

"So why tell me then. I am not interested in your story." says Socrates with finality and the matter is over.

I looked at Baloo and said, "Since you asked me for something new, I will give you some information which I have gathered only recently. In the vernacular, 'to murder' has only one name. It is *Khoon karna (to kill)*. But the English language does its best to confuse the world and thus it has many words for murder. If you murder your brother, it is '*fratricide*'. If one murders the sister, it is '*sororicide*'. If one murders the husband, it is '*matricide*'. If one kills the wife, if it '*uxoricide*'. If a child is killed, it is '*infanticide*'. If you kill a race or an entire nation, it is '*genocide*'. If you kill someone intentionally, it is '*murder*' and if it is unintentional, then it is '*manslaughter*'. If you kill yourself intentionally, it is '*suicide*' otherwise it is an '*accident*'. Finally, if you kill one or both parents, it is '*Parricide*! There is a word for suicide in the vernacular though and that is '*Khudkushi*'!"

"Go slow, my friend! These are too many words in one sentence. How did the thought of murder enter your mind suddenly, Doc?" Baloo interrupted.

"You know what the Turks did in Turkey in the olden days? They had Sulphur baths which were medicinal in nature but in a corner of the spring, there was an area which produced a gas from the sulphur. They called it the suicide corner because the gas was poisonous. When a person got too ill, the relatives would take him to that corner and make him inhale the gas. Naturally the person died. Now is that murder or assisted death which they term as Euthanasia these days?" Teji had just returned after a fourteen day holiday in Turkey after travelling 4500 kilometers. Apart from getting tired, he ended up an encyclopedia on Turkey!

"While waiting for the two of you, I got down to reading an article about the Pakistani who was killed by a group of Punjabi boys in a fight over the sale of illicit liquor. S.P.S. Singh Oberoi, a business man and hotelier of Dubai heard about this and decided to help these boys. He then paid the entire sum of 1.2 million dollars blood money out of his own pocket for the other people backed out at the last moment. It is a fantastic gesture, especially for an Indian. That is how I got down to the word 'murder'!" I replied.

"Haan, haan! He contributed the bulk of the blood money collected by the Punjabi community of Dubai." Baloo clarified.

Teji suddenly burst out animatedly and said, "No, Sir! You are sadly mistaken. S.P. Singh Oberoi is a personal friend and I know for a fact that the newspaper report is correct. No one else contributed even a single paisa. He donated the entire sum from his personal account.

He does not keep a single paisa of the interest that he earns on his income for himself. He donates the entire amount for various causes and he has been doing this for years. It probably would run into crores of Rupees."

Teji stopped to see the effect of the information he has just disbursed on us.

I had my mouth wide open, while Baloo's was shut, very tight.

Teji apparently was satisfied with our response, for he carried on, "And you know, he has married off almost 18,000 poor girls out of whom 260 were Muslims and Hindus?" Teji stopped again to see the effect on us.

My eyes had bulged out and were on the verge of popping out of their sockets while Baloo developed a squint.

He carried on, "He has opened a school for challenged children in Patiala. The entire building and running of the school and hostel is on him." Baloo hadn't spoken a word since his initial comments.

"How well do you know him?" I asked.

"Once while I was returning from Zurich, I stopped over at Dubai. I wanted to pay my respects to him. I was of the opinion that visa was granted on arrival. To my utter bad luck, I found out that it wasn't. I was stranded. I rang him up and was shattered when he told me that he was in Chandigarh. I told him about my predicament. He advised me to wait where ever I was and that someone would contact me within 10 minutes.

After 10 minutes, two burly men dressed in black suits came, asked me if I was Tejbans and when I confirmed their fears, they picked up my luggage and asked me to follow them. I protested saying that I will carry my own luggage but it did not seem to affect them. They escorted me through a route which appeared like an obstacle course and suddenly, I found myself outside the airport. There was a fleet of cars waiting. Someone put my luggage into one of them. I was escorted to another and the cavalcade snaked through Dubai to his hotel.

I felt like a Don for the day.

They took me up a lift which opened into a suite. It was like a football field, with six rooms and a huge bar stocked with the widest range of liquour that I had ever set my eyes on." He again stopped for effect.

"Doc, anything that you could ever imagine was there. I was shell shocked. I told one of the people attending on me to take me to a smaller room, something that I could afford. He replied that they had been specifically ordered by Mr Oberoi to house him there and that I was free to have anything to drink from the bar and order anything that I might want to eat. Mr Oberoi called me a little later and asked me to make myself at home. He would be arriving at six p.m. the next day. I went around the city trying to while away the time till he arrived. Back in the room, with so much booze surrounding me, I could just sip a few and then went off to sleep in a huge round bed. The next day arrived and so did Mr Oberoi. He arrived at precisely 6 p.m. as promised. The rest is another story. So? How well do I know him?"

I was excited. I mean, real excited. A shiver ran up my spine in anticipation.

"Can you arrange a meeting with him? I want to write about him in this book. Do you think it is a good idea?" I asked not wanting to stop to even breath.

"It is a very good idea. He is the right man to be written about in the book. I will call him later in the day and see what his program is."

I had serious doubts about the fruition of my meeting with Mr Oberoi. Why would he want to meet me? My doubts were laid to rest when Teji rang up to tell me that my meeting with him had been fixed for the 4th of August!

"Wow!" I said and thanked Teji profusely for the effort.

He replied, "Mr Oberoi never answers my call when he is Dubai. He always rings back immediately. I told him about you and that you wanted to write about him in your new book. He is coming to India on the 3rd and will see you on the 4th."

I was too excited. After all, he was the first celebrity multi-millionaire I was destined to meet.

I began my wait for the 4th which was only 3 days away but it seemed like an eternity. I was again informed that there was a change in plans and Mr Oberoi had to go to Patiala on urgent business. He would see me on the 6th. I had no other alternative but to wait, though, impatiently for the 6th, armed with questions that I had for him. I realized that I had met him fleetingly twice before. The first time was at Teji's 60 birthday bash for which he had come all the way from Dubai. The second time was when we attended his father's bhog ceremony in Mohali. But those were fleeting encounters. I doubted if he would remember me.

I got another call from Teji on the 6th that Mr Oberoi was in town and wanted to know where we should meet. I suggested my house, the golf club or Gelato. He agreed to come to Gelato and talk over a cup of coffee. He asked me to reach Gelato in ten minutes. I quickly collected my dictaphone, extra tapes, extra set of batteries and reached Gelato. I thanked God that there were no people sitting on our table. Teji was already there, somewhat tense.

The two of us sat and did what has to be done under the circumstances. We waited. Five minutes later Teji received a call. Without saying anything to me, he got up and left only to return within two minutes. He has with him *the* Mr S. P. Singh Oberoi.

I noticed that Mr Oberoi wasn't a very tall man. He had an open smile. His upper eyelids drooped over the outer angles of the eyes which give them a hooded appearance. I put his age in the 65 to 70 bracket.

His skin was not smooth. It was what we would call 'weathered'. If he was working in the rough desert conditions of Dubai, it had to be weathered. I was wrong. My guess about his age was off by a decade, for when I asked him his date of birth as we conversed, he informed me that he was born on the 13th of April 1956, on Baisakhi day! That would mean he was just 56 years old.

As a reflex, I blurted, "Ha! Compared to me, you are a child. You are seven years my junior and you have achieved so much in life. I have not even started and my time to depart is almost upon me!"

I was delighted by the moustache that he sported for it was more impressive than mine. It was the kind of moustache which would maintain its' shape till the owner wanted it to be different. It had a complete twirl because of which the ends turn into the mainstream after a full circle. This is the picture that you see of the eye of a hurricane taken from a satellite. A very significant habit of moustache owners is that they start giving their own moustaches a good twirl the moment they see one which is more impressive than theirs. I don't do that normally because it is very rare that I came across a better one than mine. But that day, I realized that a strange desire, nothing like I had ever known, arose from somewhere deep inside me, to start twirling my moustache. It would have been disastrous! I quickly controlled my index fingers and the thumbs from their impending action thus saving the day.

He had a maroon colored turban, the size of which was a shade on the larger side. It covered the outer angle or canthus of each eye which only exaggerated the hood of the upper lids. The eyes were sharp. They took in the coffee shop quickly and then rested on me. He blinked his eyes frequently because of the turban coming low over them. He smiled and shook my hand as Teji introduced me. I offered him my seat. At first glance he was dressed simply in just a plain shirt and pant. There was nothing to indicate wealth. His shoes were simple. I saw no branded stuff. I was totally wrong again. He wore only Marks & Spencer shirts. His trousers were always Raymond Suitings. He had an AP hand crafted gold watch. I asked him to take it off and let me see it on a later meeting. When he did that, my eye balls reacted the way they were supposed to . . . . they attained the size of golf balls, and popped out only to zip back in again with a twang. For crying out loud, even the thick heavy strap was made of gold. It was very rough finish as if to give an impression that it was raw gold. He had a collection of 75 such watches, he informed me casually. He had a Mont Blanc ball point pen in his shirt pocket. Since I was on the subject of prized possessions, I later asked him about what else he liked to collect.

"Mobile phones! I love to collect mobile phones. I have about 25 of them and I keep changing the SIM cards when I want to use a particular one. I have a running feud with my wife who just can't understand why I need so many of them. She wants me to give them away. My favored one is the Tag Hauer set of mobile phone and wrist watch."

Maybe he saw a suspicious look in my eye so he added quickly, "There are three things which I never give away."

"And they are?" I asked

"My mobiles, my pens and my watches!" he said.

Why am I not surprised after hearing this? My brain was screaming silently, "Ask him about his collection of women and if he gives them away or not. The Arabs call such a collection a harem!" I knew there will never be a right time to ask him about his harem, now or ever! I would just have to shoot from the hip and find out myself.

That morning, as he took out his visiting card, I noticed that even his wallet indicated the owners' loyalty, for it had obviously seen better days. His mobile was on the vibratory mode. It began vibrating in a soft purring sound the moment he put it on the table. It started on a journey as if it had a life of its' own. Mr Oberoi responded to each call and replied very cordially in a soft voice which was almost mesmerizing. I noticed no gruffness which was so commonly seen in well to do men wanting to show off their status.

Teji started off by exaggerating about how great a doctor I was. Not satisfied with himself, he went on to say that I was the *best* doctor in the world. Obviously, he hadn't seen enough doctors. Or, maybe he did not know that there were other people who had taken up this business of healing too!". Then he exaggerated the number of books I had authored. He put the figure at 12! I did not need to interrupt. I could have repeated the usual cliché dialogues with an embarrassed expression, "No, No jee! Teji has a habit of exaggerating!" and I then could have looked at the floor, blushing in all shades of pink. I did nothing of the sort. I just sat there with a smile on my face and looked at Teji with an amused expression. I noticed the same phenomenon when we met again in the evening at the Chandigarh Club. Mr Chaman Sharma, who is Mr Oberoi's tax consultant was there, and he went one step ahead. Teji had made me an author of a dozen books. Chaman made me an author of 15 books.

The way things were progressing, there were chances that I might even have beaten Agatha Christie by the time the evening was over!

I realized that the time had come for me to take over. I started my tape recorder. I had tested it before his arrival.

"Oberoi Sahib! It is a pleasure to meet you. I am writing a book about the happenings in this small coffee shop and the people I meet, the conversations that I have with the younger crowd and some of the stories which develop here. One day, not too many days ago, I was reading a newspaper here, while waiting for Teji to arrive and saw the news item which described your heroic attempt to help out in kind and money to the 17 boys from Punjab who had been sentenced to death by hanging in a Sharja court. Teji and I got talking and another friend said that you were responsible for a part of the money raised by the Punjabi community of Dubai?

Mr Oberoi interrupted me with a bit of head nodding, "No! No one from the Punjabi community contributed anything."

I went on "Teji has already refuted that statement and has gone on to regale us with tit bits about your philanthropy. I was very impressed and wanted to write about you in the book. This is purely because you became the subject of our discussion in the Gelato Coffee Shop! That is why I requested Teji to arrange a meeting with you here. Thank you so much for coming. I am also very excited because you are the second celebrity whom I have met in my life!"

"Badi Khushi di gal hai ji. Pucho, jo puchna hai!?" he happily replied (It is a matter of immense happiness! Ask me what you want to ask.) "Just a matter of curiosity," he went on, "who was the first celebrity?"

"Ah!" I replied shyly, "That is a long story. She was Priya Rajvansh, the Bollywood actress"

He smiled.

"Sir, I don't want to include you into the book because you are a rich man, or because you have donated 1.2 million dollars for a cause and people start calling you a philanthropist or because you own a five star hotel in Dubai. I want to include you because you are all the things that I have elaborated plus the fact that you a real humanitarian. You went beyond the call of duty. You not only paid the blood money for 17 people, but you fought for their lives. You got the 'revenge' changed to blood money and helped 17 families who would have been shattered and on the road to hell! That is why you qualify to be included."

"First of all, mine is not a five star hotel, it is just a four star hotel. I am the head of the hotel which is called 'Dubai Grand". It was started in the year 1998. It has 147 rooms, three Delux suites and one Presidential suite. My favorite place in it is the Sher-E-Punjab Dhaba!"

"The difference is just a swimming pool, isn't it?" I asked.

"We have a swimming pool. But it is rated as a four star hotel only." he replied.

"Why did you get so involved in this case?"

"When I first came to know about this case which involved 34 children of my beloved Punjab, the thought that struck me was the shameless injustice of it all. If one Pakistani was killed in a fight, how can someone justify the hanging of 17 boys in that connection? That was what hit me in the beginning. Suddenly, all kinds of politicians from Punjab descended upon Dubai, trying to help these unfortunate boys. They failed for they did not belong to the region and just wanted mileage out of the case without knowing the customs of the people of Dubai or the parents of the boy who was killed.

Once I decided to get involved in it, these do-gooders disappeared. They had had their fill of publicity." He stopped and looked down on the table as if he was remembering the past.

"Then it was up to me to hire lawyers for them. My trips to the Punjab began in earnest after that. I visited every family of 34 boys who were in the jail in Dubai, for various offences. They included the 17 who were sentenced to death. That took me to every nook and corner of Punjab. What I saw will remain with me forever. Their families were in a pitiable state. These boys had sold off their land, their houses and had taken loans so that they could pay the people who would send them to the golden land of Dubai. What they earned was hardly enough to repay their loans, and survive Dubai. Sending money back to their homes was out of the question. So these workers had to resort to selling illicit alcohol and if they could sell three to four bottles a day, they could easily make more money and hope to repay loans in two years. Initially, the laws of the land were lax. If they were caught, they would be let off after a few months in jail. Hence they were not scared and risked getting caught. The same was with the Pakistani boys. Conditions prevailing in Pakistan are even worse. They also wanted to clear their debts. It was a simple matter of the stronger group controlling the trade and making more money in the business. Thus there were frequent brawls between the Pakistanis and Indians, since these were the two major groups."

I was listening with rapt attention. So was Teji. The telephone vibrated at intervals making a purring sound, making the mobile phone dance from one location to the other, seeking his attention. Once he finished talking on the mobile, I carried on.

"Obviously, you could not do much for their families." I said.

"I felt so much sorrow for them. In one case, I met the prisoners' wife who was carrying a one year old infant in her arms. I asked if her mother-in-law was also there. She replied in the affirmative. When I asked to see her, four people brought her into the room on a cot. She was totally paralyzed and could neither move, speak or respond. After her son left, she resorted to washing utensils in other people's houses. When she heard the news that her son was to be hanged, she suffered a paralytic stroke and that was the end of it all. I reached the conclusion that till the time their boys don't come home, the thing they would need most to survive was money. I decided to send each family 4000 rupees every month. So now, each of the 34 families receives a cheque of that amount every month and they will continue receiving it till their boys come home. It has been two years."

"Wow!"

"The real problem in front of me was the on-going judicial process. One had to be involved in it every day of the year. I neglected my business. There was no help from any quarter. You said that the Punjabi community helped in collecting money. Let me tell you that not a single paisa was donated by anyone in Dubai. One would think that people in India are so poor that no one could donate money for these 17 people either. It wasn't that. The real reason is that Indians have no compassion left in their hearts. Everyone is so involved with themselves that the other mans' suffering has no effect on them."

"Sir, in India, there are thousands of people who are rich but they cannot donate money for a cause. In Hyderabad, they have an auction for the right to pour milk on the Mahavir statue. They wash the statue once every 12 years. Last time, a person paid one crore and thirty six lacs for the right to be the first to pour milk on the statue! I don't know how much milk he poured or how many people could have benefitted from that milk and the money, but he did it only for his own superstitious benefit. God knows that the Mahavir temple doesn't need money. Philanthropy has a weird meaning for us Indians. Even in National calamities, we give 1-2 thousand rupees and feel very proud of our generosity, forgetting that many a time we have spent more on whiskey in one evening. I am the same. And even then, we are worried if that money is going to be tax deductable or not." He had touched a raw nerve in me.

"Maharaja Amarinder Singh, his wife Rani Praneet Kaur and Mr Sukhdev Singh Dhindsa were the only people who helped us as intermediaries with the Pakistani authorities, the parents of the slain boy and the judiciary in Dubai. They were the people who helped in getting 'revenge' out of the picture and instead of 'blood for blood' we got a plea of 'blood money'! Then it boiled down to how much we could bargain. Even there, these two with their Pakistani friends intervened and finally a figure of 9 crore Pakistani rupees which is 4.5 crore Indian rupees, was settled upon. This sum was something that that the 17 boys could never have collected. They simply did not have it. I volunteered to pay 2.75 crore INR and hoped someone else would pay the rest. No one else came forward so it was up to me to put up the entire 1 million dollars, which I did.

On top of everything else, when things were going in our favor, the Indian press brought out stories that these boys were being mal-treated, their hair had been chopped off by the prison authorities and many other lies. The infuriated judge showed the newspapers to me and wanted to know who brought out these stories."

"Here I am trying to help you, Sardar Sahib and Indian Newspapers are printing this rubbish about us!" he admonished.

Now, I had another problem on my hands. For that, I got the parents of the 17 boys to Dubai, arranged them to meet their wards and in a press conference, each boy was presented with hair intact and their stories that they were being treated well by the prison authorities. I paid for the fare of the parents, made them stay in my hotel and succeeded in clearing the air."

I could only repeat, "WOW!" another time.

"So what happens to these boys now?" I asked.

"They have completed most of their prison time, so they will be free sometime in October or November of 2012. But they can never come back to Dubai and neither can they go abroad for any job. The authorities in Dubai are very strict about their laws now!"

"What did you feel when you were writing the cheque for that big a sum?"

I asked.

He replied as a matter of fact, "To tell you the truth, I did not feel anything. I felt as if I was just an accountant of God and He was asking me to write that cheque and deposit it in court!"

"You did not feel any sense of loss of your hard earned money? About how long it took you to earn the stuff?"

"No. When I am thinking about money, I think only about the 392 rupees that I received as my first pay in my first job. I gave the full amount to my mother. That is the only money which is important to me. Subsequently, I have earned and spent millions. God gave me that money. It was never mine. So if I give it away on His command, what special thing have I done?"

"Yes!" I conceded thoughtfully, wondering how many of us would have that kind of a thought process. "It is the way ones' mind works. Most of us think that *we* are the ones who have earned our money by *our* hard work. Oberoi Sahib, tell me how you ended up in Dubai?"

"That is a very interesting story. I was working in a construction company in India and we came to know that a company from Dubai was hiring workers. The interview was to be held in Hoshiarpur. The first bus to leave from Katara for Hoshiarpur left at 4.30 a.m. Katara was 46 kilometers from Riasi, where I lived. I discussed this with my friend Mohinder Singh. By the time we reached the decision that we could not make it to Katara, it was already past 8 p.m. and pitch dark. Somehow, I had the feeling that I should go for the interview. So I told Mohinder Singh that I would go to Katara alone if he wasn't willing to join me. He asked me how I intended to reach Katara when there was no bus for that day. I explained to him that Katara was just 46 kilometers away. If we started walking then, we could reach Katara in time to catch the bus to Hoshiarpur in the morning.

Against his better judgment, Mohinder Singh joined me. I have already told you that it was pitch dark. The fear factor was there. That was a hilly area. The whole place was full of fog. It was so thick, that one could probably cut through it with a knife. I wanted to cut through and open a door, hoping it would be bright and sunny on the other side. But it was only a fantasy. It was as foggy on the other side as it was on ours and wherever we turned our eyes! Like two blind men, we tapped out the road, for there were chances of going off it on a different route.

We took turns reciting various prayers like Chaupai Sahib, Japji Sahib etc (Sikh scriptures) on the way which kept us distracted from the dark and fatigue.

21

Can you imagine? We walked 46 kilometers during the entire night. We were so scared. That kept the fear away and we never realized that we had walked 46 kilometers and reached Katra, and in time for the 4.30 bus. We reached Hoshiarpur absolutely tired but happy that we had made it for the interview. I was the last one to be interviewed and was selected for the job. Unfortunately Mohinder did not make it. He came to Dubai later though. By then I was fairly well established in my business. Despite my repeated requests, he never joined my company."

"Why didn't he join you?" I was astounded.

"It could be pride. I think that he felt safe in the comfort zone of the company he was working for and the steady salary that he was getting. With me, there was always a certain amount of risk involved. He was not adventurous as I was. He is still working in Dubai on the same salary. But he is happy and we are still friends."

"And then?" I asked.

"I worked in Dubai as a mechanic for four years and then came home to join my father in Talwara. The company was called "Pritam Singh & Sons". We constructed roads, canals, dams, a 1000 km link road, bridges and a railway line. This was the only railway line which was built after independence in those days and it ran from Beas to Govindwal!"

"Wonderful!" I said. The only thing that I did not do was to give him a standing ovation.

"So when you were doing so well in your company, why did you go to Dubai again?"

"I went back to Dubai in 1993. You can call it destiny. I was working on a construction project in Dubai. The British engineers faced a problem with the sandy soil. They were not sure if the pillars that they were constructing would take the weight of the building for a prolonged period. I told them that I knew how to do it. They ignored me for I was just a mechanic. They kept trying on their own but failed. I persisted till one of them agreed to test me out. They did not have Hydraulic jacks which could take that much weight. I knew someone in India who could make them.

They asked me about my future plans and how I was going to get the jacks. I told them that for the jacks, I needed to go back to India and see someone in Yamuna Nagar, a sleepy industrial town in Haryana. I even suggested that they could deduct the expenditure of my visit to India from my salary.

They agreed with my proposal. I landed in India and immediately went to Yamuna Nagar. I knew there was a company called Oriental industries which specialized in such jacks. I sent in my visiting card. The owner Mr. Lalit Saluja made me wait for a long time in his waiting room. When he finally called me in, he wasn't very impressed by my appearance. I explained to him that

I needed Hydraulic jacks of capacities exceeding 1000 tonnes.

He said, "Sardarji, it will require a lot of monetary investment which might be difficult for you."

I asked him, "How much are you talking about?"

"It would be approximately 50." He said. The figure broke my heart.

I replied, "I can collect 25 lakhs only!"

He broke into a guffaw and said, "No, no, no, Sardar Sahib! You misunderstand me. I meant 50,000 rupees and not 50,000,00 (50 lakhs)!" Please keep in mind that in those days, even 50,000 was big money."

I was a hugely relieved man and I explained my requirement and soon we were in business. Mr Lalit went up to 1500 tonnes, then 2000 tonnes and finally we reached 5000 tonnes. The jacks had to take the weight for 72 hours. If the needle showed movement then it was obvious that something was wrong with the jack in the form of leakage. When we finally got our pillars checked for longitivity, the engineers reported that the pillars would last for 500 years, if not more!

In those days, hydraulic jacks of this tonnage were not used anywhere in the world. This news spread like wild fire. I started getting contracts of my own. I also began trading in hydraulic jacks. That is how I came into construction. Lalit Saluja and I became family friends.

I continued to deal with Oriental Industries despite the breakup of the two brothers. Oriental Industries went to Lalit's brother. But that did not come between us and our friendship continues to this day. I will be going to Yamuna Nagar to meet him in the coming days."

While I was listening to this story, I was wondering at the smallness of this world. I have had the pleasure of knowing Mr Lalit Saluja and his family close to 40 years too. I made a mental note of talking to Lalit to find out his version too.

Teji suddenly woke up, "You know Doc! He has, till date arranged 18,000 marriages for poor girls, 270 of them were from Muslims and Hindu families!"

I looked at Mr Oberoi. He got the hint that I would like the story from the horses' mouth.

"We give each couple dowry worth 30,000 rupees. It has 21 items which includes cash, a double bed, a sewing machine, a steel trunk, quilts, mattresses, 7 suits for the bride and other house hold items. Once, we solemnized 170 marriages in a single day, which is a record in itself. Food is also arranged for every one present for the ceremony."

My brain was working overtime. It was calculating. 18,000 multiplied by 30,000 is 5.4 crores! Add to this, sundries. What is this man? The word 'crore' seems to have no relevance to him. Even if the money is only the interest earned on his own funds, it still is his money. And I have always been told that if you respect money and not squander it on people, it will stay with you and probably attract more of it. He threw it around on people and still earned more.

"Are you not adding to the population woes of this country?" I laughed, "Because every man who gets married, irrespective of his financial status, has to prove his manhood by impregnating the woman he has married. He can come up with another 10 reasons why he got married in the first place and then why he went on to produce five children whom he could not afford?"

"These girls would have no home to go to if they were not married. When I get them married and they set up house, they get a semblance of respectability and belonging for the first time in their lives. This also prevents them from entering the flesh trade, because men are basically predators. They would use these unfortunate girls in any way they can."

I agreed with Mr Oberoi. It was indeed a good deed. But the way I saw it, within a year, or two there will be a sizable number of little clones of human beings running around. I saw people from well to do families not wanting to produce children. Or even if they do, they have one or two. The plea was that they cannot afford more. Then how could these people from low income groups who could not even afford to get married, afford to have 3 or more of them? Was it all because of the largesse of their hearts? I thought that they had accepted the fact that they were not duty bound to provide them with designer clothes and shoes and they might just land up in some government schools if they were lucky. Sending them to medical or engineering colleges was a dream which was too distant for them. The immediate benefit of having a large number of children was that each of them is capable of adding some money to the family kitty by working petty jobs.

"Teji tells me that you got an exact replica of the Taj Mahal constructed in Dubai?"

Oberoi Sahib laughed, "Yes! It was exactly 75 percent of the Taj Mahal in size and 100 percent in attributes. Each inscription on it was replicated though out the gardens, canals, and everything else was 75 percent of the original size. We got artisans from India for that job."

Later, I rang up Lalit Saluja to find out what all he could add to Mr Oberoi's story, his wife Anita Saluja who was listening to our conversation in the background, joined in.

She said, "S.P. is like a brother to me. I will tell you the story how he ended up making a replica of the Taj Mahal in Dubai. As usual, S.P. was with his friends, drinking to glory, and one of them dared SP and asked him.

"What special thing can you do with all the money that you have?"

S.P. expansively boasted, "I can build the Taj Mahal!"

His friend taunted him and S.P. took him on and said, "Yes. I can! It starts tomorrow!" The bet was sealed with spit on the palms and a firm hand shake. The bet was on.

And the plans for the Taj Mahal started the very next day. Mr Lalit Saluja told me that the Government of Dubai had allotted him land for the construction of the Taj Mahal. The land was for a limited period of time for the Dubai fair which is an annual affair. After the fair, Mr Oberoi would have to dismantle the entire construction. He built the entire structure to a scale of 75 percent of the original Taj Mahal. It was a colossal task which included getting artisans to choose the marble, some marble like material, wood for the floors, and inscriptions were inlaid into the marble as they were in the original. It was finally opened to the public.

There was twist in the story. The Dubai fair had to be scrapped because of three reasons. The first was the tragedy that befell the Royal family. Second, there was a record rainfall that year. The fair got washed away. The number of visitors who came to the fair was not enough. Mr Oberoi had calculated that he would make up his money from the entrance fee that they would charge from the visitors The third reason was that the Taj Mahal was there only for a limited period of time as per the contract. It had to be dismantled piece by piece. It had cost him a lot of money, but he took the loss in his usual carefree attitude.

"It was just a bet." He laughed it away.

During a discussion with Teji, I raised a point about the choice of the monument. The Taj is considered a bad omen by a section of Indian society. Marble replicas of the Taj Mahal in homes as artifacts for display are frowned upon for they are supposed to bring bad luck.

"There is a rumor that the Taj Mahal Hotel in Las Vegas might be renamed because it is running in losses." Teji informed me.

Mr Oberoi's capacity to drink is legendary. When I asked him, he was a bit shy.

"I was only 13 years old when I started drinking with my great grandfather Sardar Teja Singh. My grandfather Sardar Harnam Singh was a tee-totaller, who never drank alcohol but was very fond of non-vegetarian food, especially mutton. I was 19 when I was staying in the hostel because my father would not let me stay with my relatives for he felt that they would spoil me. At that point of time, my great grandfather was 101 years old and my grandfather was in his eighties. On many days, the two of them would walk down to my hostel, hand in hand, supporting each other because my great grandfather wanted to drink with me and both of them wanted to have meat in the hostel. One day, while returning home, a bull hit my great grandfather and he fell down. He was critically injured but he refused to see a doctor.

He asked my father to call me, "Palli nu bulao!(call Palli)"

Someone from the family rushed over to my hostel and told me the story. I was very close to my great grandfather, almost like a friend. On hearing the news, I came sprinting home. I stood before him, huffing and puffing. He did not have to say anything to me for we could communicate with each other with our eyes. He looked at me and nodded once. I immediately understood and ran to the kitchen, poured a stiff shot of Rum and gave it to him. He gulped it and dropped dead!"

"Didn't the family give you a hiding?" I asked.

"Why would they do that? It was a last request of a dying man. I just fulfilled it. He died in peace. But I learnt how to drink from him. He used to tell me to have four drinks till I am 59 and then two after I cross 60 and then carry on till my last days."

He was known to start drinking at 9 in the night and then go on till 3 or even 6 in the morning, but as you know stories tended to get exaggerated as they pass from lip to lip, exactly like the number of books that I had authored. It was also known that he would reach absolutely fresh in office at 9 a.m.

"Which is your favorite drink at present?"

"Dimple. I just love Dimple. Otherwise, it was Black Label Johnny Walker."

"Doesn't so much alcohol harm you?" I asked in awe.

"No! I got my liver laminated!" he joked "Actually there is a funny incident about the time when Lalit Saluja came to visit me in Dubai. I was always very fond of cooking. I told Lalit that we will have a couple of drinks while I cook the chicken. Lalit had his doubts since he was leaving for India in the morning. I assured him that we will only be having two drinks. But by the time the chicken was ready, we had consumed more than a bottle each. I remember telling him that I will drop him at the airport in time for his flight. Then I slept. I got up hurriedly and looked at the time. It was nine a.m.! Lalit's flight was to have left at 4 in the morning. I felt very guilty. I quickly dressed and went out in search for Lalit but he wasn't in his room. The guilt went up two notches. I rang him up and found out that he had already reached India and was relaxing in Yamuna Nagar. I apologized profusely that I overslept and could not drop him to the airport. I was curious how he managed to get up on time and catch his flight.

"Sardar Sahib, you woke me up on time and drove me to the airport. You were in your full senses. I was not, because a funny thing happened on the plane. As soon as I sat in my seat, I went off to sleep. The next moment, I felt as if there was an earthquake. It turned out that the air hostess was shaking my shoulder rather roughly and in turn I rudely told her that I did not want any lunch and that I did not want to be disturbed."

She said "Sir! You will have to get up and get off the plane. We have landed in Delhi and all the other passengers have already disembarked!" I quickly got up and sheepishly disembarked."

Mr Oberoi went on to say, "I was so shocked at my behavior for I had no recollection of anything. That meant that I woke him up, drove him down to the airport myself for I did not have a driver in those days, came back to my house and slept off!"

But whenever all of us got together, this incident came alive and we always had a good laugh. Everyone knew of my drinking. Once when we had a party, I got three bottles of Dimple Scotch whiskey. My mother knew that we would finish all of them so she rolled one in a sheet and hid it under the bedding. Almost twenty five years later, when my hotel was being inaugurated, she brought out the bottle and gave it to me.

"Do you remember this bottle?" she asked.

"No!" I replied.

"This is the bottle I hid that day 25 years back because I knew you would drink all three of them if you had them. You did finish two and then forgot about the third. You can have that bottle today!" That bottle was very special for me, he reminisced.

"Why do you drink so much?" I asked.

"Initially, I was in a group of people who drank heavily. I liked the stuff. Later, I could not go to sleep if I didn't drink. A time came when I just could not sleep, with or without alcohol. So I just kept drinking."

Mrs Anita Saluja, Lalit Saluja's wife told me later, "S.P. is the saddest man I have ever known. His younger son was not well, and the thing that bothered him most was that he could not do much about it despite all his money. He has opened a school for handicapped children in Patiala. That was prompted by his son's condition for he could only make his life just a little more comfortable and with the institution, he knew that his son was being properly looked after. That is why he drinks so much."

To bring up a topic which had already given him so much pain, was a difficult decision. But many attempts to bury that aspect failed, for it kept cropping up in my head. I plucked up enough guts and decided to ask him. That day, we were in my clinic. He had arrived in Chandigarh only a few hours ago and was in town for a few hours only. I offered to meet him in Sector 5 where he has a house. He decided to come to my clinic instead.

"Your younger son is not well?" I asked gingerly, after the initial pleasantries.

"Yes." He replied. His head was down and so were his eyes which were focused on my table for we were sitting in my clinic. He was not angry at me for bringing up a painful subject.

"Was he born that way?" I asked.

"No, no! He was a normal child. Just like any other. He fell down from the bed while sleeping. He suffered a head injury and we rushed him to the hospital. We were informed that he would need immediate surgery. They took him into the operation theater while we sat in the waiting room for the operation to be over. We were shocked when they brought him out just 15 minutes later. We asked about the operation but the nurse just dumped the child into my lap and hurried away. The child was totally inert. My son looked quite dead to me. It turned out that the doctor also had thought the child was dead. They had panicked because the anesthetist had given him a double dose of anesthesia. We were in shock and laid him on the bench. Suddenly we noticed movement. He was alive. We tried to contact the doctors but they were not to be seen anywhere.

The surgeon and the anesthetist had left the hospital from a back door and did not return for a month to the hospital. My son improved with time. I wasn't about to forget the incident that easily. They had run away. Moreover, he had not even needed the operation. A compromise was reached with the doctor and only then did they resume work in the hospital. It was later, as he grew up that we noticed certain behavior changes in my son. We were advised not to send him to school. So we hired tutors and tutored him at home. Now he can use computers and looks after himself but he gets very angry sometimes." I was sure that he wasn't telling me the whole story.

"I was told that you were very saddened by this episode and your aggravated drinking is a fall out of that."

"Maybe. I don't know." He said thoughtfully, "My main problem was insomnia, as you call it. It is only on Fridays that I get myself massaged in the morning and then I sleep for a few hours and relax. My drinking hasn't affected my liver yet. Actually, I was very fit when I was young. In those days, we did not have automated vehicles. We either walked or cycled to wherever we had to go. I must tell you that I was a bicycle maniac, absolutely unstoppable. Just to give you an idea, we would cycle all the way from Talwara, where I lived, to Jullundar only to see a movie and then cycle back. Talwara to Jullandhar was 100 kms! But our record of cycling in a single day was when we went from Talwara to Hoshiarpur via Jullundhar to see a movie and then cycled back to Talwara, all in a day. The distance that we covered was 240 kilometers! I can do a lot of cycling even today." And he gives me a smile and something to think about, something to chew on what a person can do if there is a will. That in a way is a great indication of a man's character.

"You must be exercising on a cycle in your gymnasium these days! Which cars do you drive?"

"I own a Porche, an X5, an X6, a Mercedes 500, but my all time favorite is the Sports model Range Rover. It feels like you are riding a lion!" and his eyes light up under the hood.

"Sir! What was your childhood like? Your eyes still have a naughty look about them." I asked.

"I have already told you about the drinking. Once I was accused of having indulged in the national past time of eve-teasing. My father first thrashed the life out of me. He wasn't satisfied with that. So he tied both my wrists with a rope and then put each palm under the foot end bedsteads of the old huge beds that we had in those days. He then jumped on the bed and pretended to go off to sleep." He said with a giggle and then carried on "My poor mother was wailing outside the room through the night, but there was no sign of pity in my father. He tossed and turned the whole night while my hands were under the bed posts. In the morning when he untied me, my hands had swollen up like bread loafs. They had developed large nodes in them. The nodes healed just a few years back. I can tell you one thing. I was never accused of eve teasing again. It is a wonder that I have not been turned off women completely."

"Did you actually tease some girl?"

"I might have. I don't remember for that wasn't important. What was important was the lesson." And he smiled at the memory.

"My father used to trust me completely with all money transactions from a very young age. Once, I took all the money lying with me and went away to the city with my friend. We returned after 15 days when the money finished. It was my mother who was annoyed but my father never said anything. He still let me handle the family money, against my mothers' advice. He told her that I have learnt my lesson and that I will never repeat it and in fact I never did."

"Were there any other pranks that you would care to remember?" I asked

"Once when my father returned from work, he asked for me and the servant told him that I was in the fields, gambling with my friends. My father got so angry that without even drinking water, he turned around, picked up a thick stick and headed for where we were busy playing cards. We were completely unaware of the impending disaster. My friend saw my father approaching like a tsunami. I got up and ran. He ran after me. He realized that I was faster. So he flung the stick at me. It hit me on my leg and I fell. He then caught hold of me and dragged me home. After the usual beating, he gave me an ultimatum. One of us will be out of the house by a particular date." He stopped, as if he was reliving that bashing.

"I thought he was joking. After all, which father is so cruel that he would turn his own son out of the house just because of a bit of friendly gambling indulgence? But when the day arrived, he asked me about my decision. Would he have to leave the house or would I leave? I told him that this was his house. He should stay. I would leave. As I reached the door, he asked me if I had any money. I had about 200 rupees with me, so I answered that I had enough. He called me back and gave me a thousand rupees and asked me to come back into the house only when I have succeeded in life. I was 16 years old then." As he finished the story, his eyes were focused on a distant planet, as if he had been transported back in time to that fateful day. I didn't disturb his reverie either. Suddenly he came back to the present and realized that I was still there.

"I have never touched a pack of cards after that incident either!" and he smiles again. More than his lips, his eyes do the smiling. "But I did not go home for a long time after I left."

"I believe you adore your mother?" I had been given this inside information by Mrs Anita Saluja.

"Yes! Every son does that. But if you ask me who do I worship, the answer would be, my father!"

"Why? You have always been on the wrong side of him. Remember the hands and the nodules, the beatings and how he kicked you out of the house?"

"*That was his duty as a father. He taught me to be adventurous and to have the courage to take risks in life.* Whatever I have been able to achieve today is all because of what he taught me. In 1983, I took heavy losses. I was into construction of canals. I had taken loans from people. Obviously, they wanted their money back. I got so depressed that I refused to venture out of my house. People whom I had borrowed from started coming home. I refused to meet them.

My father asked me, "What is your problem?"

When I told him the full story, he pepped me up and said that the money would be arranged. Since the amount was so large, he had to sell off most of what he had, and that included my mother's jewellery. I told my debtors that everyone would get half of what I owed them because I wanted to put the rest of the money back into the business.

My father insisted that I pay them in full. Can you imagine what those very people whom I owed money, did? They put their money and their trust back into my business and I started the canal work again. I made a profit of 16 lacs which was a huge sum in those days. That started me on the road to success. The beatings were just his way of educating me."

But when he wanted me to go to college to study arts, I put my foot down and refused. I wanted to learn mechanics. So I joined the ITI after my matriculation and got a diploma in Tractor mechanics. I had been offered a scholarship of Rs 120 (an impressive sum in those days) but my father did not let me avail it. He said that the scholarship is going to corrupt my mind. He wanted me to do the course as an ordinary student, not as a day scholar but as a hosteller! He thought that my mother would spoil me if I stayed at home. That is how strict my father was. Not only that, he was almost maniacally strict about what we should eat and drink. He was a milk buff, if there was one. If it had been only milk that he forced upon us, it wouldn't have been that bad. Milk mixed with fish oil was standard. I can't even begin to tell you how terrible it tasted, but we had no say in that. We just had to pour it down our throats. We had a lot of hens at home and we had to have four raw eggs every day. It all felt bad at that time but retrospectively thinking, these two things gave me all the vitality that I enjoy today."

"So what is happening now?"

"Before I tell you that, do you remember the Jessica Lal murder?"

I am perplexed at the sudden shift. I reply, "Yes."

"She was to join my hotel in Dubai. She could not do so because she was murdered a week before her joining date!!" he said with a shrug and looked at me, searching for my reaction. "I knew some people involved in the case because they belonged to Chandigarh. That case already has produced some loud reactions from the press and public alike. A film producer went on to make a movie of it too. The perpetrators have been sentenced."

There was a break in our conversation because it was obvious that the two of us were thinking about the same thing but our thoughts were different.

Then suddenly, Mr Oberoi came back to my earlier question. "I noticed that we as a community are very misunderstood in Dubai because of our deeds. People think that all we know is to fight and spill blood. I wanted to prove that we are much more than that. If we can spill blood, we can also give blood. In the Gulf, during the months of Ramzan, people are fasting. Hence very few people donate blood which leads to an acute shortage of blood. So I organized a Blood Donation Camp in my hotel. There were more turbans visible in my hotel in Dubai than even Punjab. Sikhs came in hundreds but the hospital authorities could cater for only 160 units of blood! Everyone was given free food and milk by the hotel. The disappointed ones were sent back with the assurance that we would shortly organize another camp where 400 people would donate blood. That camp is being held shortly. The local press gave us a lot of coverage and we can see that the impression that the locals hold about Punjabis is changing. My mission now is to revamp the Punjabi image all over the world, but more so in the Gulf."

After our meeting he went back to organize another Blood Donation Camp. But even this time around, the hospital authorities could not cater to all the people who had come to donate. They had only 250 kits. Nevertheless, there will be no shortage of blood in the blood banks of the region. Most of all, there is realization in the locals that if there is ever a shortage, there will be enough Punjabis to donate their blood for those who need it. Mr S. P. S. Oberoi has made sure of at least that.

"What else is happening on the social front?" I asked.

"I am very happy about another aspect of our work in Dubai and Sharjah. I am the founding President of an organization called "Sarbat Da Bhala". It is a registered organization and we have 250 members. I am very thankful to Mr M.P.S. Bedi, the Indian councilor to Dubai for helping us getting registered and all the help we needed in regards to the activities that are conducted under the banner of 'Sarbat Da Bhala'."

"What are the activities that you promote?" I was intrigued.

"We have 50 people working in the organization who are called 'sevadars'. They are divided into 10 groups and they teach the new entrants to the gulf about the prevailing local laws, so that they do not get into trouble looking for easy money. We have set up "Modi Khannas" in Sharjah and Dubai where people from any nationality can get free rations for at least 15 days. They also teach Gurmukhi and Gurbani Kirtan (singing hymns from the holy Granth Sahib scriptures), Gatka (traditional Sikh martial arts) to children and adults alike. You might be amused to know that we have sponsored a Kabaddi team under 'Sarbat Da Bhala'. We plan to send Gatka and Kabaddi teams to India to take part in competitions!"

I noticed a certain sense of pride while he spoke of 'Sarbat Da bhala'. It is perfectly understandable, under the circumstances. It is his baby.

"I must tell you that I am finally being honored by the Punjab Government on the 15 of August celebrations in Amritsar. But before that I will receive the Dhyan Chand Award in Delhi on the 7th of August. Then Mrs Sheila Dikshit, the Chief Minister will honor me in Delhi on the 3rd of September. On the dias, there will be four other dignitaries along with me. Mr Hooda, Haryana CM, Mrs Sheila Dixit, Delhi CM, Mrs Mohsina Kidwai, and Mr Jagan Nath Paharia, Governor of Haryana. I am the Chief Guest along with Mrs Dixit.

The President of the Rashtrya Ekta Andalon, Mr Buta Singh will honor me in Delhi."

"It is raining awards finally!" I can't help exclaiming.

He is even prouder as he lists out the awards. He has a list of hundreds of awards and recognitions from all over the world. No matter what anyone has done or possesses, it ultimately boils down to recognition by the powers that be. Recognition is the final mortal frontier. The way I look at things, in my book, Mr SPS Oberoi has done it, not because of the recognitions, but by his deeds! On the other hand, Mr Oberoi does not mind the recognition at all. In fact, he loves the adulation. After a point of time, one gets convinced that he deserves all that and more. And I wonder, why not? That only makes him a mortal and not a demi-God. The internet is plastered with photos of him inundated with garlands.

I got a call from Mr S.P.S. Oberoi on the 4th of January 2013. He was in Chandigarh and wanted to see me. He informed me that he had read whatever I had written about him. He was satisfied but there were some factual errors which he had marked for me to correct. He owned a sprawling bungalow in sector 5. I entered the gate and was received by a handsome six footer who introduced himself as Sachin. We went up a ramp to the first floor and then through a maze of corridors to a huge room where Mr Oberoi was waiting in the company of five people, who seemed to have nothing in common with each other or Mr Oberoi. As I was greeted by Mr Oberoi, they discreetly left the room. He instructed Sachin to fetch the papers from his car.

"You know, Doctor Sahib, this boy Sachin was also sentenced to death by hanging in Sharja. I have got him out of there and hired him as a caretaker of this house. You can interview him some day." And he laughed.

"In a section of the Dubai press, someone wrote that I only help people from Punjab. That is not true. Out of the 54 people on death row, 39 were from Punjab, 2 were from Hydrabad, 1 was a Gujrati, 1 Bihari, 4 Pakistanis and 4 Bangla Deshis. Of the 17 boys who were pardoned, for whom I paid 1.2 million Dollars, 16 were from Punjab and 1 was from Haryana. 750 airline tickets were issued to people of all nationalities, including those from Sri Lanka when they were stuck in the Emirates because of shortage of money, lost pass-ports or any other reason. Moreover, when someone dies, many times one has to help out with the arrangements to send the body home. My duty includes that too and there we don't differentiate the origin of the deceased person."

Yes. I thought it was indeed a matter about which we rarely give a second thought. Who looks after unclaimed dead bodies? About Sachin, I thought here was a man who owed his life to Mr Oberoi. I was keen to get a peep into his thoughts. What would a dead man walking feel once he was no longer a dead man walking. I had never really met a man who owed his life to someone in the real sense. As I was pondering over this, I was woken up by a shrill telephone ring. Mr Oberoi talked to someone in Dubai and told him that he was in conversation with Doctor Chadha who was writing about him. He suddenly said, "Here, talk to him!"

I was taken aback. A thick deep sonorous voice came clearly on the mobile phone. "Salam Valeykum, Doctor Sahib. I am Baluch of Baluchistan. It is a great deed that you are performing by writing about Mr Oberoi, because people like Oberoi Sahib grace earth once in a century. This, I say, despite being a Muslim. I must tell you that since I am the senior translator in the court of Sharjah, I am always present in the courts. Every time Mr Oberoi enters the court, the five judges look at each other and then they smile. They know that the presence of Mr Oberoi in their court means that on that blessed day, one more person will receive the gift of his life." He says exuberantly and then adds, "I am blessed, for I am his friend."

After Mr Baluch had got over his adulation of this Indian, and with promises of a meeting in the near future, he hung up. Mr. Oberoi told me a very different aspect of the problem in Dubai, Sharja and other countries of the Gulf. Expatriate laborers tended to lose their passports, overstayed and frequently ran out of money for their tickets to go back home. They were naturally sent to jail to rot.

"I get a lot of help from Maharani Parneet Kaur who is in charge of the Ministry of External Affairs of India. I have set up a ticket counter in the jail itself and instructed them that no person from the Indian subcontinent should be behind bars because of ticket problems. They are to issue tickets immediately and bill them to me. Passport issuance is speeded up because of the Indian High commission staff."

I was staring at the man. You would be too, if you had been there.

That day, was the 12th of February 2013. Overly, there was nothing very great about it, one might observe. But there was a wave of happiness sweeping over the land of Punjab, at least in the house holds of the 17 youth who were condemned to death by hanging in Dubai. On the12th of February 2013, they landed on Indian soil, with their necks intact, all because of one man. Mr S.P.S. Oberoi. They should have been free a long time back, but then the two Pakistani men who had been injured in the fight woke up to the fact that they could also squeeze something out of the situation. They did and once that was out of the way, these boys came home.

I received a phone call from Mr. Oberoi. He told me that they were a short distance away from the Darbar Sahib (Golden Temple) in Amritsar. The families of the boys had already reached. Once they offered Ardas and thanksgiving to the Lord, they would go their respective homes."

"So! You have finally done it, Sir!" I am ecstatic. "You are indeed blessed and so are the ones who come in contact with you. I read the news in the newspapers. Now that these people are free and alive, what else do you have in mind?"

"Oh" he said "this is the beginning. There are 84 boys in the jails there. 54 are on death row. 4 Pakistani boys are in jail for 40 years each; there are 10 others for 25 years each, out of which 8 are Punjabis and 2 are Pakistanis. There are 4 Bangla Deshis, 1 Srilankan and one from Hyderabad. My work is not over yet. Moreover, something has come up in Nepal."

Nepal? I was confused so I asked him when he was expected to be in Chandigarh, for I needed an update about Nepal. When I met him again, he told me the following story:

A group of Sikhs approached Mr Oberoi that he must do something in Nepal too. The Raja of Nepal had gifted 200 acres of land to Guru Nanak. The deed said "to be used by Guru Nanak as he deems fit. He can grow vegetables, do kirtan or whatever else he would like to do". (A copy of the deed was in Oberoi Sahibs' possession.)

"I could not control myself and went to Nepal. On talking to people there, I found that the Raja had indeed gifted the land. But out of the 200 acres, only four and a half acres remained. The rest had been usurped by people. They feared that this land would also be taken away. There was a Gurudwara on that piece of land which was being looked after by a caretaker. I sought an appointment with the Prime Minister of Nepal who was gracious enough to meet me.

"What do you intend doing with the land?" the Prime Minister had asked.

"I will build a hospital, school and a sarai (guest house) here." I said.

"And on whose name should the deed be?" asked the Prime Minister.

"It would naturally be on Guru Nanak's name. It is His land."

"You know, I have very fond memories of Chandigarh. I used to study in the Panjab University. Anytime we would run out of money, we would go to the Gurudwara for langar. I have many Sikh friends from those days!" he said.

I left the palace with the assurance that the work will be done.

As I went back to the Gurudwara, I noticed a round structure full of mud. I asked the caretaker about it. He informed me that it was a small well, called a 'haudi'. It had been filled over with mud.

I asked him to get the mud removed. I was shocked by what I saw as the digging went down deeper. On the inside wall of the well, Path (Sikh scriptures) was inscribed in the cemented wall!" and he showed me pictures on his mobile phone. The Sikh scriptures were indeed engraved.

"I was in for a bigger surprise. As we reached 20 feet, pure Amrit (holy water) sprouted from the well. I was aghast. I tasted it and it was the sweetest drink that I had ever tasted. I ordered the walls of the well to be raised so that the well was protected from extraneous pollutants. I then got pipes into it so that the Amrit could be supplied to the whole of Khatmandu. Just imagine, after 435 years, it was ordained that this work should be completed by me. I felt a wave of humility seep through me. I asked for another appointment with the Prime Minister. I showed him the pictures."

"So what do you intend doing now?" he asked, somewhat shaken.

"Sikh pilgrims have a lot of problems when they go to Guru Nanak's birthplace in Nankana Sahib in Pakistan. There are a lot of diplomatic hassles. Once this news spreads, all the pilgrims will be diverted to Nepal."

"And what will you do with the income that is thus generated?"

"It will naturally go to Nepal!" I said.

"There is another thing. We have about a 1000 orphans. What can you do for them?"

"That is no problem. Sarbat Da Bhala will adopt them. We shall house, educate and feed them in the school that I am building. They will study till any level they want to. They can become doctors, engineers or lawyers. We will pay for their education."

The Prime Minister was satisfied. We took over 50 children to begin with. The next time I went there, they greeted me with a chorus of, "Wahey Guru Ka Khalsa, Waheguru Ki Fatey!". The teacher I had hired had taught them 5 paudis of the Sikh scripture. I was so happy."

"Sir, suppose the local Nepalese object to the children being converted to Sikhism. They might even harm you like that fellow Dara Singh who burnt the family of the Christian cleric?"

"That is no problem. We will hand the children back to them and tell them to do whatever they feel like with them!"

At the last count 100 Nepali children have been adopted by Sarbat Da Bhala.

As I was recounting things that I had written about Mr. Oberoi, Jaspreet Nijjar, who is a Principal Correspondent in The Times Of India, opined thoughtfully, "He is indeed a great man. I personally don't know about anyone who would have done all this or even contemplated doing all these things, single handedly. But by the end of it all, one should realize that he is human."

"Why do you say that?" I asked

"Recognition! Every human being who does something or even wants to do something, is aware of what he is bound to get out of the whole thing, be in terms of money, fame or awards. Mr Oberoi has done so much for people everywhere, but he now wants recognition. He has so much money that he doesn't care about it. It is only to be recognized by the same society to which he given in plenty. Never the less, nothing is taken away from his contribution to the down trodden"

"Yes, I suppose you are right." I replied. "He told me once that he had talked to Non Resident Punjabis and asked them to send just 15 $ to a family or an individual that they will adopt. When the time comes, they will be given a name and a bank account where they should deposit that money in whatever denomination which suits them. Sarbat Da Bhala will have nothing to do except to give them logistical support. This way, no one can possibly mishandle money. When the time comes, Mr. Oberoi is sure he can collect crores of dollars without having any direct relationship to the donor or recipient."

There is a village in Punjab called Maqboolpura. In a short span of time, 550 men died because of addictions. They left behind 372 widows in the age group of 25-40 years. They have 750 children between them and no one to look after them. They have a Mr S.P.S. Oberoi to look after them now. He has opened a school for them and provides books and uniforms plus a yearly grant of Rs.25,000. 550 of these children have gone in for higher studies.

4 girls from Talwara Girls High School have come into merit list of the state. Sarbat Da Bhala will pay for the studies of these 4 children to any level that they choose

for themselves in any stream. So far, Sarbat Da Bhala has sponsored 475 students for higher studies in fields like medicine, Engineering, law etc.

He then looked around and found that hundreds of people died in accidents in Punjab during winters. One big reason was the lack of reflectors on cycles, tractor trailors, trucks and buses. With the help of Patiala District police, he has distributed 50 lack radium reflectory stickers in 27 districts of Punjab.

Punjab, like other states lags behind in eye care. Mr Oberoi held eye camps, where 1100 cataract operations were performed. Lenses and medicines were distributed free. The aim is to get 5000 operations done next year.

This man's work needs to be recognized by the world. I suppose God broke the mould after he created Mr S.P.S. Oberoi. Every man has detractors. I am sure Mr S.P.S. Oberoi has his share of them too.

May God bless whatever project he has in his mind. He hasn't even attained the age of 60 yet. I am just wondering which mountain he plans to move next. By the way, today is the 12 of Feb 2013. It is one year since the 17 youth came back to their loved ones.

CHAPTER 2

It was one of those days when I was absolutely free. I did not expect any patient for the rest of the day. When one has been practicing for as long as I have, one sort of develops intuitive knowledge about these things. We call the winters 'healthy season' because the number of patients dwindle down to a hurtful level for some practitioners and gives me time to write.

That was the day when Sam Panwar rang me up to find out if I was free for coffee. His full name is Shamsher Jang Singh Panwar. I like long and tortuous names. It gives the owners a certain regal character. Long names also sound good to the ears, almost like tags of royalty. As a quirk of fate, God had given Sam eyeballs which were always at an angle of fifteen degrees from the horizontal. That gave him a 'superior than thou' look for he seemed to be in direct communication with God at all times. That look also doubled as a look of extreme boredom when it suited him. When I met him, he was en route to balding. Such people tend to grow a beard or a 'goaty' to balance the loss of the hair on their heads. But Sam, who was a 'cut surd', (which means that he had shorn his hair despite strict religious orders not to), had decided to sport a beard. This decision of his to cut off his hair can easily be mistaken for a trait of revolt in his character. Overall, the balding pate, the tip of which reached six feet two inches from mother earth, the eyeballs at 15 degrees to the horizontal and the beard with a pointed end, which is a trademark of Arabs, gave him a very aristocratic Arabic look. It went

very well with his long, winding, never ending name.
But we called him Sam.

Sam was a much travelled retired corporate honcho
who had recently returned from Bahrain and Kuwait.
Anyway, we were 'drinking and golfing' partners, Sam
and I, amongst other things.

*The crux of the matter is that one can never play golf
with a person whom one doesn't like very much.* One
can play with someone who is not your type, once;
maybe another round if one is that hard up for playing
partners, but one can never carry on playing with him
for more than 20 years! I liked his company, for he,
without realizing, taught me many things about life. I
tended to listen to him because he also happened to be
8 years my senior.

*One of the things that I learn from him is to laugh at
everything which is thrown at you, to take the good with
the bad, and the happy with the sad.*

It is like you are playing bad golf and you still end up
getting a birdie when the ball that should have actually
gone out of bounds hits a tree and lands two feet from
the pin! He laughed when he duffed or shanked his
shot. No one is expected to laugh when one misses
a two foot putt. Sam does! In short, I can proudly say
today, that, finally, my thought process is as warped as
his. Almost, that is.

*Somehow, I have stopped seeing the world as the world sees
itself. The two of us always saw the funky side of it all the*

*time, at least till the time we were together. It got worse as
we approached the nineteenth hole. (The bar in every 18
hole golf club is called the 19th hole).*

With this history, how could I refuse the chance to have
coffee with him?

He was not a born Panwar, but a Sekhon. For some
reason known only to Sam's father, he changed his
surname to Panwar after being commissioned. He was
a part of the British army in the Second World War
which was captured very early in the war while fighting
the Africa Corps under Field Marshal Rommel. He
was subsequently sent to Italy as a POW in 1941. As
the story goes, two other officers, Kumarmangalam
and Yahya Khan were also there. They later rose to the
rank of General in the opposing armies of India and
Pakistan. In addition to planning an escape, Lieutenant
Panwar proved to be a linguist, mastering the German
and Italian languages. He and two Yugoslavian Colonels
escaped and were given shelter by a group of equally
hungry gypsies.

Sam is always unendingly thrilled and untiring while
telling the story about the time his father was on the
run after escaping from the POW camp. The only
edible things that he and his friends came across in the
forests were carrots and turnips. Mr Panwar had always
thought himself to be a great cook of Indian food. He
offered to cook a dish of carrots and minced turnips to
satiate the hunger pangs of the group he was with. The
dish turned out to be so utterly and completely inedible
that both, the famished escapees and the gypsies,

collectively decided to stay hungry and die rather than eat that dish. Sam laughed every time he reached the part where his father's culinary master piece found itself thrown unceremoniously into the wayside ditch. It was covered with mud, lest it be discovered by some horrified Germans or even some hungry animals.

They would have been thoroughly disgusted with the human race just because of the dish if not for anything else.

The year was 1942. It was then that he met up with Mr. Subhash Chander Bose of the INA. He was probably one of the first officers to join Bose and was elevated to Colonel Panwar. Somewhere during his stay, he overheard the conversation of Mr Bose with the Germans where he found out that Bose had decided to leave for greener pastures in the far-east without blowing too many trumpets. Bose left in a German submarine for Malaya. No one has heard of him since though stories about him and his whereabouts are still in circulation. Sam's father treaded over the treacherous Alps on to Rome in 1944 and was given refuge in the Vatican till the American Army arrived to free them.

Back in India, he was betrayed by an Indian officer to the British that this was a man from the INA and not a POW. Sam's father was arrested and housed in the Red Fort in New Delhi. They were looked after rather well with a regular supply of beer with trimmings. It is in the Red Fort that Sam first met his father, accompanied by his mother. The year was 1945. He was four years old. Sam still remembers his father was having beer when another group of I.N.A. officers were brought in. The British housed only officers in the Red Fort. Curious, Sam's father and the rest of the people went out to see who the new arrivals were. Sam at the age of 4, decided to polish off the tankard of beer which had been thoughtlessly abandoned by his father. Soon, the party arrived back only to find young Shamsher running around the central pole of the tent, banging into whatever obstacles that came his way, completely sozzled.

That was a fine start to a promising drinking career, which is happily continuing till the writing of this book. He can still have 4 or 5 drinks if someone twists his arms adequately. Sam is 70 years old.

Sam was a kid of about six years in 1947, when the partition of India took place. I had heard many stories of the killings that took place during the partition of India but he was the only one I knew who had actually seen someone being killed during the riots. As Sam and his mother travelled from Lyallpur, (now in Pakistan) they had witnessed gruesome sights of hundreds of dead bodies lying along the road. Whereever people of the two communities came across each other en route to their respective countries, fighting broke out between them resulting in people getting killed by the thousands. This happened everywhere, along that route. Sam's mother held a handkerchief full of Eu de Cologne to Sam's face to mask the stench.

Sam's father made arrangements for them to stay at the Majitha house in Amritsar. Sam was at the gate when an army convoy came to a screeching halt in the deserted market place, raking up dust. The convoy was ferrying a collection of scared Muslims, nervously heading for Pakistan. A man got off the truck to get some water. He was easily recognizable by the henna colored beard and the cap that Muslims wore. Before he could collect whatever he needed, the convoy moved off, leaving him behind. He was noticed by a Sikh gentleman sitting in a roadside shop.

In an instant, he came running out with a naked sword in his raised hand, shouting "I have lost my entire family in Pakistan killed by your people! I have no one left. There is no way that I will let you go back alive, you dog!"

I think that venomous shriek would have been enough to curdle anyone's blood. The victim, who had nothing to do with whatever happened to the gentleman's family being killed in Pakistan for he was here in India when those events were transpiring in Pakistan. He had a petrified look in his eyes for he knew what would happen next. Never the less he tried to make a dash for it, but the Sikh gentleman slashed at him repeatedly as he ran after him, till one swipe almost separated the head from the body, and blood spurted from the open wound like a fountain. Sam looked on in awe, rooted to the ground. The Sikh gentleman then dragged the body into the compound of the adjoining building, which was a mosque, and dismembered the body by cutting it into pieces. His mother heard the yelling and rushed out to see Sam looking on impassively. She yelled at him to get indoors but Sam had seen so much of killing and death already that he said, "Don't worry, mother! It is just another Muslim!"

That statement sums up the thought process of those times.

Before reaching Amritsar, they were on their way to Moga in Punjab, where Sam's maternal uncle resided. They arrived at the Ludhiana railway station. Sam was in the waiting room of the railway station when a train steamed in. Before Sam's mother could stop him, as any curious kid will do, Sam walked onto the platform to see what the commotion was all about. A train, full of slaughtered Muslims had just arrived on it's onward journey to the newly formed Pakistan. Some of the dead were hanging out of compartments. Others were lying dead inside, brutally massacred. There was one person who had some life left in him. As he moved and groaned, a Sikh gentleman noticed him. I wonder if he qualifies to be called a gentleman for, so great was the hatred for each other at that point of time, that instead of helping him or giving some water, as was the custom of the Indian sub-continent, he shot him dead with his rifle. Sam was watching.

This was reciprocated to Indians living in Pakistan. There were hardly any villages left in Pakistan which had any surviving Hindus and Sikhs. The ones who survived were those who had changed their faith by becoming Muslims. That is why there are so many Pakistanis today with Indian surnames. The ones who thought that they were lucky to have boarded trains and were on their way to a new home were murdered and these trains arrived in India from Pakistan, full of massacred Indians. Most of them were hacked to death.

The hatred was equal on both sides of the newly created border.

Maybe, memories of those incidents are what really goaded Sam to slaughter me on the golf course years later. And I don't even look like a Muslim!

He made his first Muslim friend, in Calcutta many years later. After that, most of his friends in Kuwait, Bahrain and other places were Muslims and quite a few of them were from Pakistan.

If man did not have a short memory, he would become crazed like some people who did not want to forget.

I was born in 1949 in Mumbai, then known as Bombay. I don't blame the British for our own foolishness. Our ancestors participated in the killings. No one was forced to kill neighbors. The killings in Punjab and Pakistan were real. They might seem to be just forgotten stories of an era to Indians living in other states of India and other countries. But the horrors were such that anyone who qualifies to be called a human being, of any nationality and who has a semblance of a brain, would never participate in riots again. But apparently, killing has been ingrained into the human brain. We did it again in 1984, 1993, 2002 and 2013. Children were cut up, and pieces shoved into the mouths of their mothers, just like the Moghuls, hundreds of years earlier, had forced Sikh women to wear body parts of their children around their necks as garlands. In 1984, they put burning tires around the necks of innocent Sikhs all over India and burned them alive. At that point of time, only Sikhs died, for they were not allowed to retaliate by the police. But the next time this happens, I am afraid many people will die on both sides.

The way things are going, we will do it again and yet again. Time and again, India and Pakistan have needlessly fought wars over Kashmir and have nothing to show in terms of gains by either side. We have destroyed families of the two countries and we will do it again. The vultures are still circling in the skies, for they know that food will come their way. If for nothing else, someone will throw a carcass of a pig in a mosque and a cow's head in a temple and thought will come to naught! Man is the same everywhere. From the concentration camps of Nazis in Germany to the concentration camps of Bosnia, this is what happened. A soldier offered a bowl full of gouged human eyes to his superior officer who accepted it as a bowl of grapes! They cut off the limbs of their neighbors and hung them on the walls of their drawing rooms as trophies! They made humans eat their own excreta. No one will learn.

Anyway, Sam took up after his father and grew into a tall gangly lad. His race against gravity ended at about six feet two. He was always been into sports. For the uninitiated, Sam is a Sikh. He was working in Kolkata where the Sikh influence in those days was minimal. Hence he and his friend missed out on the fact that it was Guru Nanak's (founder of the Sikh faith) birthday on that fateful day when Sam and his friend decided to get their hair cut. So they happily jaunted into a hair saloon called 'A. N. John hair cutting saloon'. Sam told the receptionist about their decision to dispense with their long unshorn hair. The proprietor, Mr. John who had seen the two Sikh boys come in, insisted on looking after the two gentlemen personally.

When he was out of hearing distance of the others, he confided "I am no A. N. John! I am Amar Nath Jain. But if the SGPC (the governing body of Sikh affairs) comes to know that on Guru Nanak's birthday, the two of you have come to get their hair chopped, I am sure they are going to get nasty."

The two felt sheepish that they had missed such an important date for the Sikhs, but since the decision had been made they went ahead with the change of scenery on their heads. But it seemed to me that he had taken a decision to carry on tying a turban when the occasion demanded it, so he continued to keep a neatly trimmed beard handy. This way he could tie a turban and look like a Sikh when he wanted to and at other times, go without one and blend with the crowd. He felt he had the best of the two worlds. But ever since I have known him, he has never flaunted a turban.

Personally, I think he would look very handsome with a turban. He also does not have a paunch and that is why Sikhs are considered the fittest martial race in India. Sam behaves like a pucca gentleman all the time, excepting when he is with me. Maybe, being married to a senior army officers' daughter and being associated with personalities whom I would never mix around with, had made him a little too warped for my comfort. When in each other's company, they tried outdoing the other in the business of name throwing. In this contest, I am usually lost for I don't know any big names. The ones that I knew were from news channels of TV. This art came automatically to people who have been educated in public schools. My classmates seem to be lost into the quagmire of time. Their names have been buried deeply into the sulci of my brain.

Sam was married to a lady with contrasting tastes. One (Sam), could devour meat of any kind if the need arose and the other abhorred non vegetarian food. One was a pure sports freak and the other one had never dabbled in anything which is remotely connected to sports. As the oft repeated story goes, once Sam was asked to drop Bishen Singh Bedi, *the* famous cricketer, to Feroze Shah Kotla Stadium in Delhi. After a quiet breakfast in Sam's house, they got into Sam's car with Bedi lugging his gear. They had to pick up Sam's wife from a friends' house.

After the preliminary introductions, she asked Bedi, *"So you play games?"*

Bedi did not know where to look. Neither did he know if he was coming or going! He had taken 4 wickets the day before while playing a test match against the mighty Australian team and was splashed all over the newspapers. Sam frantically searched for the keys of the car which he had suddenly dropped. One cannot expect Bedi to have forgotten those 4 words in a hurry.

But as human beings, the two made a wonderful couple and delightful hosts.

It isn't that I have liked Sam from the first moment that I set my eyes on him. In fact it was quite the opposite. It was a very strange string of weekends for we didn't have a full four-ball. We were only three of us. To play a three-some on a winter weekend is like being the most unpopular golfers in the club. Can you imagine not being able to muster another measly person who would like to play golf with the three of you on a weekend? It is as preposterous thought as any. But that day, the truth was that there were only three of us. The marker pointed to a tall fellow with a strange gait, a strange hat, the cornea floating at an angle of 15 degrees to the horizontal as if he was practicing Alfa meditation in motion. He seemed to be almost floating around. In fact he was looking for a game as desperately as we were. The only vital difference was that he needed three people and we needed only one. The first impression that we got was that we would be better off as a threesome. We rejected him on the flimsy ground that he looked like a bore and maybe a snob too. We did not know that he had recently decided to make Chandigarh his home town and thus he knew very few people, let alone golfers.

"He is a good player!" remarked the marker. This information was blocked by our respective tympanic membranes. We ended up playing a three-some.

Wonder of wonders, the same sequence of events repeated itself on the next day. It was a Sunday. Our regular fourth was still nursing a sore back. The only person available was the same gentleman we had the audacity to reject on Saturday. We were duty bound to reject him again. After all, by sheer logic, a man cannot become interesting overnight! A bore and a snob had to remain a bore and a snob! This sequence was repeated on the Saturday next week as well. It was providence that we were fated to play golf with this man as the fourth member of our four-ball. So we invited him to join us. Our behavior had not missed Sam's attention. Moreover, true to my habit, I confessed the truth after my third beer. Despite all that, we played together for more than 10 years till the fateful second heart attack and what it did to Sam later on.

Sam was extremely well travelled, and had worked in many countries and was the most humorous person I had come across ever since I had begun to grow up. The process of growing up continues. He could recite all works of P.G. Wodehouse *ad verbatim*. He had imbibed humongous amounts of all kinds of alcoholic and non alcoholic drinks that have ever crossed his path. He had eaten stuff that I would choke at the very thought of. Obviously, his sexual escapades are not to be discussed here. His family was under the impression that he had stopped smoking 30 years before his first heart attack. But don't we know better? Some of these golfers lit a cigarette on every tee and would finish it before they began putting. Sam had done the same thing before he suffered his first heart attack. Luckily or unluckily for him, his family had problems with their olfactory nerves. The odor of the tobacco that he was so happily inhaling and exhaling did not reach their brains. Thus, they missed vital clues and never came to know the truth. He was graced by two heart attacks which were not in the least, unexpected.

The first one had come in the middle of the night when all phones, including mine were down. Those were the pre-mobile phone days. I came to know of the heart attack the next day when his father in law got through to me. The second one happened in Tokyo, when he was visiting his daughter some years later. This one cannot be blamed on cigarettes for Sam had stopped smoking after the first heart attack. This definitely is a fall out of his smoking days.

I am not sure if it was just the smoking that caused him to have his heart attacks. When I was trying to graduate from Medical school in Shimla in the early seventies, during exams my friends would make a curious decision. All of them would study in my room. I didn't object since there was nothing much to object, really. On the contrary, it seemed to me that they wanted to do that only to show how popular I was. I missed the point completely. They wanted to study in my room only because they did not want to make their own rooms untidy. They had my coffee too which I was supposed to keep replenishing as the night wore on. The silver lining was that I was forced to stay awake as I made those endless cups of coffee.

As the night jogged along and the clock steadily carried on doing what it was supposed to do, the number of cigarettes that these people smoked also went up. They performed an awe inspiring act which they called chain smoking. If I remember correctly they were not supposed to let a cigarette go out. The next one had to be lit with the stub of the one about to expire. Soon, my room was so full of smoke that I was no longer sure who was sitting next to me. It seemed to me that the smoke screen was so thick that I could slice through it with a knife. It was a great surprise that we could read the words written in fine print of our thick text books. This was repeated every couple of months when an examination was announced. I ended up inhaling a lot of secondary or 'passive' smoke.

40 years later, none of those smokers have suffered heart attacks as predicted by medical pundits. I was the only one who ended up with three stents in my coronary arteries! I have never even touched the stub of a cigarette! By the way, the oft talked about and notorious cancer of the lungs has bypassed all of them. The 3 trillion oxygen free radicals that each cigarette is supposed to generate also decided to give them a pass. The only people of my class who are dead are dead only because some of them **chose** to die by committing suicide. Some others died in accidents. None of them died because of the cigarettes that they smoked!

Life is like that. Someone else does something wrong and still gets to enjoy life while fools like me suffer irrelevantly.

That is why Sam called me a Lt. General for my three stents, read stars.

Coming back to the second heart attack that Sam suffered in Tokyo, it is also a fact that Tokyo's traffic cannot be the envy of any city in the world. Now, Sam had always been a very thoughtful fellow and did not want his daughter to suffer unnecessarily. So he timed his heart attack and the subsequent cardiac arrest to the precise moment when he reached the emergency department of the Tokyo hospital *after* his daughter had negotiated all the traffic snarls of Tokyo city.

A world famous Japanese interventional cardiologist was at hand but since Sam was unconscious, he forgot to tell the doctor about the first heart attack that he got in India. The world famous Japanese doctor did what he was famous for and managed to bring him out of the cardiac arrest thing. He then wheeled him into the cath-lab and proceeded to push in a stent into the artery which had caused his first heart attack and not the one which had decided to close down operations a few minutes back. The embolus had naturally hardened with time. The artery ruptured as a mark of protest.

Blood spurted out of that artery as if his Excellency, Count Dracula, was having a rave party.

It seemed everyone excepting Sam, panicked. It was perfectly natural for him not to panic for he has played many nerve racking rounds of golf with merciless opponents and partners alike, who could easily demolish any adversary. More importantly, he was under sedation. Sedated people are not known to have panic attacks, and since he did not know that his artery had ruptured, the need for him to panic did not arise at all. The good doctor hurriedly pushed two more stents into the ruptured artery and managed to stop the bleeding. The artery was then declared to be safe. And so was Sam. The doctor finally pushed one more stent into the artery which was the cause of the fresh arterial block.

Sam ended up with four stents! He became Chief Of Army Staff, Sam Panwar!

Sam was a cool dude. He was still oblivious of what was happening around him. Otherwise I am sure he would have given the doctor the information he was dying to get his hands upon. There was another problem. It seemed no one spoke a word of the King's or Queen's English in the entire hospital. And Sam didn't speak Japanese either. So, at the end of the day, even if Sam was in a state to proffer the required information in English, no one would have made head or tail of it. Oh! The cultural woes of the mortal world! In India, we call an Indian who cannot speak the Queen's English in the pro-*pah* manner, a moron! An illiterate bhaiya! But then what would we call the Japanese?

That is where the Japanese Gods floating around hospitals just for occasions such as these, came into their own. They helped Sam get better but Sam was in no mood to leave because of the beautiful Japanese lady cardiologist looking after him. Neither person could understand what the other was saying but there was a lot of hand holding and back patting, which Sam seemed to love. I would have loved it too. But it proved very good for his heart. Still, the inevitable happened and Sam had to leave for India, a bit morose but alive, so that he could play some more golf and drink some more alcohol with us.

On the first post cardiac arrest round of golf that we played with him, we noticed that Sam's golf swing was no longer the same after his stint in the Tokyo hospital. He fell back like a cricketer pulling the ball for a six. At times he also had a canine swing where he raised one leg sometime during the execution of the shot. I have not been able to time the exact raising of the leg though. Did it happen before or after he had made contact with the ball, is a question which needs more research. Sam was such a versatile golfer that he was capable of anything. He could lift his leg before or after his drive. The ball once hit, stayed hit, and then went off in any direction which took it's fancy.

He has talked to me of the beautiful Japanese lady doctor who attended to him in the hospital in Tokyo. I don't believe for a moment that the lady doctor or any other lady for that matter, could possibly change Sam's or any golfers' swing for better or for worse. A 'swing' is very much an integral part of a golfer's character and intrigue. Only the owner can destroy it, as Sam finally managed to do. Towards the end of his golfing days, Sam had almost forgotten how to swing, excuses notwithstanding. The connection between the club head and the ball was only incidental and accidental. Sometimes I would like to think that the ball, once addressed by him, just to get the misery out of the equation, would strike the club head on its' own and go off into the wilderness! Because Sam tended to go off to sleep on addressing the ball!

His wife then put a spanner into our drinking plans and announced that Sam will not have more than two drinks. A dictate like that spells doom, for what can two drinks do for a person who has never counted his drinks in his life. For that matter, any alcoholic worth the title, will forget his counting the moment the first drink is poured.

Also, counting the number of drinks is akin to blasphemy. It is a no-no thing! It can be equated almost with the Chappattis (pancakes) one has had. In good old Punjab, a hardcore Punjabi never counts chapattis while he is busy demolishing them. He uses his hand span if one has to see if the offered chapattis are enough. The satiety center of the brain is always switched off and has no role to play.

So how can one count the number of drinks? But we got around that very quickly. We first commandeered the jug of beer which kept floating in front of our eyes like a mirage ever since we turn the dogleg 17th and then shift to whisky after the beer has gone down the hatch or wherever it is supposed to go. When Sam's wife asks Sam about the number of drinks he has had, pat comes the reply, "Two, yaar! And stop being a nag!"

We never lied. That was the only pillar upon which our lives were balanced so precariously. We insisted that we have had two drinks only. It was an entirely different issue that a sin of omission is better than a sin of commission. We have had beer and then we have had whiskey. Two drinks. We live our lives so simply. It is only whiskey and beer. We just don't tell her how many jugs of beer and whiskey shots have gone in.

After surviving a cardiac arrest, do you think a bit of alcohol can undo what only God has ordained? He wants Sam not just to live but to live it up!!

But she knew us better.

It seemed to me that her looks could easily burrow a few new holes into me depending upon the angle she is staring at me from.

She asked sternly, "Doc! Was it two drinks?"

"Sure! It is just like the man says." I said, poker face and other paraphernalia in place. That is the least one can do for a friend.

And for yourself, for drinking without a friend is like being in a marriage without a wife.

"OK! Its' your life, Sam! Live it the way you want to!" and she walked away in a huff. As a parting shot she added, "The two of you are the most incorrigible people I have had the misfortune of knowing! Did you know that?" I am not too sure if smoke was pouring out of her ears?

Obviously, yaar! We have to know that much about ourselves. Incorrigibility is a virtue at our age.

At the end of the journey, we should arrive at our destination, all battered and bruised and be able to say "Wow! What a ride!" and not be nicely tucked in, safe and totally healthy, but in the bargain, very dead too!

CHAPTER 3

I was sitting in the coffee shop with Sweety Brar when Teji walked in. The moment he saw me, he laughed out loudly and then became serious.

"Doc! What is the matter with you? You look awfully sad. Did something happen?"

"Is it that obvious?" I asked. "Yesterday was a terrible experience. I was in the clinic when I got a phone from my mother-in-law. She came straight to the point. Her sister, Raju, who had come in from the U.K., had suddenly dropped unconscious. You know how I hate such calls, specially when they are about family. I dropped everything and rushed to their house in sector 16. The lady was lying on the bed, quite motionless. I didn't need God to tell me that she was already dead. But then one just can't announce somebody dead without feeling the pulse, checking the heart beat, performing cardiac resuscitation etc. In any case, predictably, the BP was un-recordable. Her pupils did not react at all. When everything was done, including a few hard thumps on her chest, which failed to elicit any reaction from her, I withdrew and stood with my head hanging low over my knees."

"And then?"

"And then what. I looked up to see ten pairs of eyes riveted on me. After being in this profession for so many years, I still find it very hard to break the news of a patients' death to the family. They were waiting for me to tell them what they already knew. I told them that she has been dead for about 30 minutes! Obviously, the timing was correct, for everyone agreed. Various reactions from the people around gushed forth. Some began to cry loudly, as if they were waiting for my signal. There were others who began sniffling. You know, our NRI relatives have relatives spread all over the country, more so in Punjab. When they visit India on holidays, they have to, as a matter of duty, visit everyone, especially the husband's relatives. Raju Masi was also on such a whirlwind tour of Chandigarh, Amritsar, Ludhiana and Ambala. I think her heart gave up due to exhaustion."

Teji was listening to me very intently, "I remember seeing her once at a function!"

"Yes, you must have!" I replied, my mind very far away. We had a nice time when we went visiting them in Torquay in England. She looked after us so well. She had presented me with a green Lamb's wool cardigan. I still have it after 35 years.

"We spent the better part of the night in depositing her into the morgue, faxing applications to the Indian High Commission in London for the grant of visas to her children and other relatives so that they could come for the funeral. My medical certificate was needed for that. I am absolutely fagged out!"

"What a coincidence!" Brar interjected. All of us turned towards him.

He was an athletic 6 foot 3 inch person with a booming voice. It was common knowledge on the golf course that when Sweety Brar laughed on the third green, people teeing off on the first tee would have their golf balls dislodged from the tee because of the vibrations he produced. Despite his size, he was still known by his childhood nickname, Sweety! He was like a fountain, bubbling with humor. You could even say that he was humor personified, though sometimes he did cross the line. His sparkling eyes gave him away even if he wanted to be serious. In fact I have never seen him serious excepting when he lost his temper and beat up some poor fellow for offending him. This happened about once in three years.

"And that is?" I wait for his answer.

"A politician friend of mine died and I have just come back from his funeral. There were more than 1500 people at the cremation. They were party workers, relatives and family. I have never seen so many people crying."

"He must have been a very popular man!" I said.

"Yes, he was a popular politician of that area. But the people assembled there were not all crying for him. Most of them were crying, believe it or not, for a langoor present at the site. People at the cremation could not hold back their tears on seeing the plight of the langoor. It was totally heart—broken and did everything from crying, howling, beating itself, throwing itself on the ground and everything else it

could do to express its' grief at the death of its' master.
I am not sure if my friend was the master, father or
mother to the langoor."

"How did your friend get to befriend the langoor?"

"It is a long story. Many years ago, my friend was
younger with habits of a man from the famed
agricultural background of Punjab. Like everyone one
of his generation, he too was fond of hunting wild
boar and partridges. Blue bull was also a specialty.
One would often see him and his friends in their open
jeep, drinking whisky and beer with double barrel guns
cradled in their arms. They were a scary sight when they
were drunk. That is exactly the scene on that fateful day
when they were driving in the Dalhousie hills. The sun
was almost hidden, as if it had been tucked in the hills
for the night. There was a nip in the air. Fog had begun
to make the area hazy. The setting would have been
ideal for some lovebirds in its' romanticism. Birds were
creating the usual cacophony of 'chi-chi-chi' noises,
which they produce when they have to settle down
in the trees for the night. I wonder why they do that,
day after day. They haven't performed earth shattering
deeds which they are duty bound to tell each other so
animatedly. In their excitement, they dirty the whole
area with their excreta. That is why it is not a good idea
to be under a tree which has been chosen by them as
their lodging for the night. But the point is, why the
ruckus?

It so happened that as my friend passed under a tree,
one of the occupants of the jeep let out a blast with

his gun, straight into the air, shattering the calm of the evening. The birds which had settled down for the night having exchanged their stories, flew out and created a louder ruckus. My friend brought his jeep to a screeching halt and began admonishing his drunk friend for the lack of understanding the basics rules of the hills. Barely had he turned around when something fell from the sky with an explosive sound just in front of the jeep. Everything around them rattled.

The occupants of the jeep were alarmed and gingerly got out of the jeep to investigate. In the dying light they saw a grey colored mass occupying the road. They went further, only to see a huge langoor lying in their path with blood oozing out from its' chest. On closer scrutiny, they were shocked to see that it was a female and was nursing a small baby langoor. My friend was shattered. He was an emotional kind of fellow. He couldn't get over it. There was no way he way he was going to abandon the cub on the road. In the mean time, the other langoors started creating pure and unadulterated pandemonium, the noise level of which was far greater than the cacophony of the birds. My friend gathered the cub in his arms and carried it to the jeep. He made a place for it, put his jacket in such a way that the shocked cub could sit into it and be covered by it also. It looked at my friend with such beautiful eyes that my friend started crying. He immediately christened it Raja, hoping that the cub was a male. Later, they realized that it was indeed was a male. They abandoned plans of a shoot and turned back home."

Sweety Brar fell quiet after that. We, on the other hand were waiting with baited breaths for the story to continue. I was tremendously curious and asked Brar, "So what happened after that?"

"You want to hear the whole story? You must be joking. I have to go to the golf club. Some friends are waiting for me." he said.

Teji pleaded with him, "Arey Yaar! We are also your friends. Finish the story. Please?"

"So Doc! You owe me a couple of drinks in the club. Agreed? I would have got free drinks today in any case."

"Done!"

Brar resumed his tale of the baby langoor, "My friend bought a baby feeding bottle, and all other paraphernalia that a human baby would need. He wasn't married so he geared up mentally to look after a baby. As it is, he was a 'gentleman farmer at large' with nothing much to do. When he reached home, he shouted for his servant, who came running out. My friend got out of the jeep in a bound and rushed to retrieve the baby. He then handed it over to the servant with great care, admonishing him all along, "Oye, dhyan naal. Mar devain ga!" (Be careful, you will kill it!)

The servant covered the baby and took it inside and shouted for his wife, who too came running, alarmed at the commotion. One look at the baby langoor and all the maternal emotions seemed to flood into the room.

She took hold of the baby as if it was made out of glass and hurried out of the room.

"I will heat some milk for the poor little thing. Where did you find him, saabji (master)?"

"Oh, it is a long story. Go bring the milk bottle. I will feed it myself."

That night and every night, my friend had the baby next to him in his bed. Every time the baby stirred, my friend got up to see what was wrong. He reduced his drinking too, so that he could be available to it. The baby langoor would hold him tight when he slept. It would refuse to be fed by the servant couple. It had to be my friend. Only when it was to be bathed would it let the servant's wife handle it. Slowly, and steadily, the baby became an infant and then a child. Its' size was definitely not proportionate to a human child.

It doted on my friend. Where ever he went, Raja the langoor, held my friends' hand and walked along. When he had to go out for work, Raja would play like any normal child at home but with one eye on the road, waiting for my friend to came back. When he came back, he would run down the road and jump into the jeep and hug my friend and shower him with kisses. I have not seen a human child do that.

Years passed and my friend got married. Raja developed a good working relationship with the bride but a problem arose when it was time to sleep. Raja threw tantrums which the servant's wife could handle with great difficulty for he wanted to continue to sleep with my friend. Slowly but surely, Raja was weaned off my friend. but only for the night. He was almost fully grown by then. Visitors could enter the house only after my friend cajoled Raja to let the person in. Even then, it would hover around, fearing the worst. Raja had grown into a strong lad because of the choicest food that he got to eat. The supply of milk was never ending. Home-made butter and ghee was the order of the day. And then one winter day, my friend gave him some rum. Raja became tipsy and his antics became so violent that my friend decided that alcohol and Raja didn't mix.

The inevitable happened. My friend's wife delivered a baby girl. Raja would not leave the baby's side for a moment. It proclaimed propriety rights over the baby and from then on, barring a few humans and their pet Alsatian dog, no one could cast a glance towards the baby. The baby grew and soon was riding on Raja and the Alsatian. But what Raja felt for my friend did not change at all. He was the father and friend. My friend had two more children along the way and Raja was the body guard for all three children. If given permission, it would have sat in their class rooms too.

When the sugar cane crop was harvested and was ready to be ferried back home and then onwards to the sugar factory, Raja would be sitting on the tractor trailer, never letting village folk pull out any sugar cane. People knew who Raja was and what it was capable of doing when it got angry. Many a times it slapped humans and dogs. The crack of the slap was heard far and wide and that deed was never repeated. When my friend's truck went about the village, the driver could not see if there was a vehicle trying to overtake it because of the load it was carrying. So he got a bell installed for the cleaner so that he could warn him. Once the cleaner went off to sleep and did not ring the bell. The driver admonished Raja rather harshly for not warning him. After the driver went back to his seat, a slap was heard widely. Raja had slapped the cleaner for he knew that the shouting he got was because of the cleaner!!

Then the day came when my friend went on the same Dulhousie road where he had picked up Raja as a baby. No one knew what happened but his car was found in a roadside ditch three days later. Anyone would have missed it unless he was off the road or looking for it in that area. Three days later, some goat-herd went after his goats which had strayed off the road and he stumbled upon the overturned car with my friend in it, very dead. The police came and pried out the body. When they brought him home, Raja went berserk for his master did not respond to its' overtures in his usual manner. Slowly, the reality of the death of his master dawned upon Raja and it went into a depression, clinging on to my friend. It would not let anyone come near the body. It was the three crying children who hugged Raja and took him away to their room.

And today, at the funeral, 1500 people cried not for my friend but for the loss of the langoor, Raja, who was my friend's son."

I looked around and noticed the others trying to avoid each others' eyes.

Brar stopped speaking. I could see the tears dripping down shamelessly down his eyes. I had always thought that he was not capable of sad emotions. For once, his booming voice abandoned him as he let out a whispered 'bye' and slid out of the parlor as if embarrassed.

CHAPTER 4

That day, I told Sam to pick me up from the clinic. We were not so lucky because there are people sitting in our chairs. My chair, if you please! We took up the other table. The door opened and a funny looking, ill shaven man with a stubble walked in as if all the barbers in the city were on strike. He was dressed in loose, ballooning BJP style brown Khadi knickers. He was wearing those cheap, obnoxious Bata fleet shoes. *He was not wearing socks!* I decided I would not want to be seen dead in his company. His hair was flowing in all directions and in addition he had a weird, lost look in the eyes. He spotted Sam and his face suddenly lit up like the fourth of July. He tiptoed towards our table. Sam got up to greet him.

"Hi Gullu!" and they shook hands, Roman style. Sam threw a lot of emphasis and inflection on the 'lloooo' for Gullu! He could have kept it short instead of going on and on and ending up sounding like an 'ullooooo!' for one could easily forget that someone had also uttered a 'g' in the prolonged ooooos.

The gentleman in knickers sat down. I noticed that his thin legs looked well fed only because of the lush growth of hair on them. It also seemed that he was wearing contact lenses. I took a closer and more careful look. His eyes were a mixture of green and light brown and it was then that I realized that those were not contact lenses. His eyes were natural green. I was beginning to change my first impression of this untidy, unshaven man with disheveled salt and peppery hair which succeeded in giving him a certain aristocratic look despite all the bad things that I noticed about him. I looked at Sam from the corner of my eyes, just to see if his taste in friends had changed along with his swing after the Tokyo episode.

"Doc! This is a very dear friend, Gullu! He is from London. We were together in Bishop Cotton School in Shimla. By the way Gulloo, Simla is now Shimla. Gullu, meet doc! He is also known as Jaideep Chadha. We play golf together, amongst other things." And he laughs which would make an observer very suspicious about the 'other things'.

"Oh! Not you too, *Jay-d*eep! You also play that silly game called *golf*? You look sen-*sible* to me." He pronounced Jaideep as *Jay*-deep. He had a British accent and my diagnosis was that it isn't a put-on job. Thank God for that. I have had enough of put-on accents. Chandigarh is full of the fake British, Irish and American accents. Even a congenitally deaf man can tweeze out the fake ones. Most of them haven't even stepped out of Chandigarh.

"Hi Gullu! My looks are very deceptive. I admit that I am completely non-sensible. And I do play golf and it makes me a complete nincompoop because I play the game with guys such as Sam here, despite the fact that his swing is no longer the same. I can safely infer from your statements that you are a non golfer? And that you are new in town?"

Gullu let out that laugh which I was destined to get familiar with in the coming days, even when he was very sad. He had plenty of reasons to be sad later. But at that moment he had nothing to be sad about. His eyes suddenly have a thousand laughing crow lines, "For the love of God, nooo! I am an old dog from the lanes of 'Chandigah'. I have a house nearby. I just flit in and out of Chandigah! This time I brought my wife, Marie! She will be delighted to meet with you!" It seemed to me that he had eaten up the 'r' in Chandigarh only because he was hungry.

"Gullu has a huge place in Sector 5. He was a great sportsman of our school. He wore the school colors in cricket, athletics and boxing. I could box a bit too but Gullu was our finest."

"Boxing? How long ago was that, Gullu? I believe you have to have strong legs for boxing?" I remember seeing his thin legs. They had seemed to me in some desperate hurry to give up carrying his weight "Gullu was so fast with his punches and hooks that he rarely needed his legs. He needed them only to prance around and confuse the other guy in the ring. But his calves were like a bulls' calves. The usual results were knockouts! So don't even think of messing with him. He can still knock people out." Sam warned me.

I had no intention of starting something that I could not finish. In fact I have never boxed. It seemed to me that boxing was a barbaric activity and all that one party wanted to do was to inflict damage on the other party as destructively as it could. I must remind you that I am not in the damaging stream of life. I am the healer. We finished our coffee over small talk.

I took an instant liking to Gullu. He was something like Sam. Both laughed without reason and incessantly. They remembered something about school and laughed. Their laughter was contagious. I liked that.

I like people who can make me laugh and are ready to be laughed at.

I found out that Gullu lived in London with his wife and two children. He was in awe of his mother-in-law who he said was a fine woman. I found that very interesting for I have rarely found too many men who appreciated their mothers-in-law the way Gullu did. He was an art critic as well as a dealer in art. He was not critical of just art, but of the artist too. All that he had to do was to stare at paintings for a long time from various angles and then act as if he was 'evaluating' them, whatever that means. He then bought the ones he thought would be appreciated and then sold them at exorbitant prices to people loaded with money. That was how he earned his living. One didn't have to be an anywhere near being an artist himself. The critic just lets other people work and then he uses big words which become bigger as he becomes a bigger critic. By then, he wields enough power to tear some artist's work to shreds or praise it to the sky. One is thus never out of work. That explained the disheveled hair! A critic has to have the 'look'!

"J*ay*-deep, it was *wonder*-ful meeting you! I am sure we will meet again. That is if Sam doesn't want me to go back to England sooner! Vera will be coming over at the end of the month!"

"And who is Vera?"

"She is my little sister. She lives in Mum-*bai*!"

"Oh! Great! Should I drop you where ever it is that you stay?" I asked.

"Oh bloody hell*! Nooo*! I love walking in In-*dia* in these silly shoes. But I love them. They are so light."

I mentally reiterated the point of not wanting to be seen dead in them. He should have at least put on a pair of socks! I found people who came in from the US or UK felt that they could dress in any way they wanted and still get away with it. Whereas, Indians in India have to be decently dressed and not move about in knickers or vests.

We walked out of Gelato. The beggar boy, Arjun, was waiting for us to come out. He had the same expression on his face. He was never sad or angry at his plight. His legs were crossed at a grotesque angle. He just hopped around using his arms as propellants. This activity has made his upper torso very powerful. I gave him a 10 rupee note. He accepted it with gratitude on his lips but his expression told me that I have not done him a favor by dishing out 10 rupees.

It is his right because God made him a cripple and made me normal. I can walk and work and he can't. In a way, he has to be taken care of by people like me. That is the rule of the universe.

This theory was also propounded by the leader of a eunuch group, after they insisted that I pay them 11,000 rupees just because my son decided to get married! I paid them what they demanded, for I am aware that they could turn very obnoxious if they were denied the money that they asked for. They expose themselves at the drop of a hat, which is very embarrassing to the onlooker. None of my family objected to the fact that we have to pay them. Moreover, since we treated them in a civil manner, they too were on their best behavior with us. They danced, sang and showered blessings on us and the house. They promised to come back when a son was born and threatened to take 25,000 rupees then. Despite that, we heaved a sigh of relief when they finally departed. The leader, by the end of it all had started calling me 'bhaiya'(brother) and my mother, "Mataji (mother)"!

"Is this a sector where sophisticated people live or what?" the leader asked me.

"No. Why do you ask?" I asked, somewhat surprised.

"We notice that all the neighbors are hiding inside and not taking part in an event which brings great happiness to your family! Arey, we have to survive after God made us into eunuchs. The duty of the normal people is to look after us. Isn't that right?" she asked.

Everyone must be shit scared that these eunuchs might decide to visit their house next, I thought.

Anyway, that day, Gullu walked towards the garden that will take him through the sectors to sector 5. Sam and I walked back to the clinic.

"Vera is Gullu's sister." Sam had the tone of reverence as he described her, "She was a 'bomb' when we were at school in Shimla. Later, she was arguably the most beautiful screen face that you may have ever seen." Sam ventured forth with his general knowledge, as we walked through the corridors of the market.

"I have never heard of an actress named Vera." I say.

"You know her as Priya Rajvansh!"

"I stopped in my tracks. "Priya Rajvansh is Gullu's sister? Shit, man! I have been watching her movies since I was fifteen years old". Sam was absolutely right. There could never be another actress anywhere in the world as beautiful as Priya Rajvansh. The modern ones are so artificial. They think that the beauty of a woman lies in the waist or there about. Sam was about 8 years my senior. Priya might have been around his age, I thought. It seemed Sam is a mind reader, for he confirmed my calculations without being asked to do so. I was 15 when I saw her in India's first modern day war epic 'Haqueeqat'. This is a movie which was made by a prominent film maker of those times, Chetan Anand, about the Chinese treachery and later invasion of India. Priya played the role of a simple hilly girl who falls in love with Dharmender acting as Major Bahadur Singh. I could still see her prancing down the hill side, pebbles rolling down, trying to keep pace with her, as she raced down, straight into the arms of Major Bahadur Singh.

One can imagine the pebbles stopping abruptly to gaze upwards as the two of them embrace.

Who can forget such a sight? At least, it seemed to me that the scene had been etched in my brain forever. As she gazed at her lover with large dove eyes, I decided that even Vijayantimala paled before her.

"What Sam! You have taken me back so many years!"

"O Blimey! I almost forgot. I was supposed to invite the two of you over to my house for drinks and dinner today! My wife would have killed me. Be there at 8 with your wife. Gullu will be there along with his wife, Marie."

"O.K." I say. With that, he went back home and I went to the clinic with stars floating in my eyes. I look forward to meeting her at the end of the month.

CHAPTER 5

Sam had invited about 30 couples for the evening. He was staying in the first floor of a 1000 square yard house which belonged to his father-in-law, a retired senior army officer in sector 33. My wife and I were introduced to Marie, Gullu's wife. She was British and appeared to be very friendly, slightly on the plumpish side with very pleasant vibes emanating from her. She had streaks of grey in her hair. She taught English to the English and whoever else wanted to learn the language, in England. We started talking and kept on talking as if we had been friends for about a thousand years. We sat down on the veranda floor with our feet on the grass, without a care in the world, oblivious of the sophisticated people around us. We were in our own world. There seemed to be no topic left which we had not discussed. We were so engrossed in our talk that we failed to notice Gullu as he passed behind us. He did not come over on the first pass.

Then as he returned, he came over and asked Marie, "Marie, is this burly Sardarji trying to rape you?" (Sikhs were called Sardarji out of respect)

Marie looked up at me. Her neck was at an interesting angle and after some thought replied, "Not yet." And then went on to add, "No, I don't think so." After another pause, she added, "I don't really think he is the raping kind!"

"Be careful of these Sardars (Sikhs). Who knows what a few drinks down their throats might turn them into!" And Gullu laughed loudly with his crow lines accentuating. Soon Marie and I joined him. When we finally stop, he said, "Hi Jay-deep! So we meet again!"

"Gullu! You are shocking, you know. In India, that would be the last thing I would have asked my wife. If I suspected someone with those intentions, I would not have asked her about the guy's intentions. I would have settled it myself!" and we laughed some more.

I was introduced to the Kissingers, a German couple during the party. Walter Kissinger had taken over Groz Beckart Asia as the Managing Director very recently. His company manufactured knitting needles by the millions! They have had an extended spell in Pakistan. They surprised me with their knowledge of the clans of Pakistan, Baluchistan and the Pakhtoons. If that wasn't enough, they went on to tell me what I didn't know about the different gotras (sub castes) of Haryana, Gujarat and Rajasthan in India and how they differed in their behavior because of the gotras. I was flabbergasted. I informed them that I was the company Doctor for Pfizer, the pharmaceutical giant in Chandigarh. He immediately became interested in me and wanted to know if I would be interested in becoming the Doctor for their company too. I was excited and agreed because Pfizer, in any case was on the verge of closing down it's operations in Chandigarh.

I circulated around meeting old and new friends. Sam's father-in-law had his dinner early. His table had been set in true army traditions. While he was having his dinner, we concentrated on drinking some more of Sam's whiskey. Sam's wife had laid out an excellent spread of continental dishes. Some of us were high as expected. At least I was. I looked around and it seemed to me that Sukhi was also very high. No thought of raping anyone had entered my brain yet. I informed Gullu about the happy tidings. He said 'Thank God for small mercies!" Marie seemed relieved.

On that happy not, we left soon after.

CHAPTER 6

Dreams and fears are not meant to come true, or are they? The last thing that I ever wanted was for Gullu's dream and Priya Rajvanshs' fears to come true. But then they did. As a result, many lives were altered.

Now you know who Gullu and Priya are. I was just that emotional idiot who got his fingers burnt because of the habit of thoughtlessly putting them where they should not have been in the first place. Priya got transported from India to England for higher studies and theater; she graduated as a Shakespearean theatre actress and decided to come back from London to India. She landed straight into Bollywood movies. She had no choice. With her looks and her training she could have gone nowhere else. Gullu's father had left a palatial 3000 square yard house in the posh sector 5 of Chandigarh for the three siblings. Gullu used to come to India a couple of times every year with his family to spend time in that house. That is when Priya also flew down from Mumbai to Chandigarh to visit Gullu, for the two were very close. Once in a while, Gullu called a few of his friends over when she came. I was always there.

As I have already told you, Gullu was married to Marie who was a British school teacher and taught English to whoever cared to learn the Queens' language. They lived in the suburbs of London. Gullu confided in me that his mother was a clairvoyant who used to get dreams which more than often than not, came true. Once, on the eve of his departure on a holiday to the French Riviera, she dreamt that he was involved in a motor accident. Next morning she told her son about the dream. She also described the damages that would be inflicted on his car and the injuries that he would suffer. She strongly objected to his holiday but he did not listen to his mothers' warning and off he went to the French Riviera. The injuries that he and his car ended up with were exactly as predicted by his mother. Priya told me that Gullu also dreamt of stuff which came true, including the last one in which Priya was involved. Priya went around telling her friends that her brother had dreamt another of his famous dreams.

If only she had listened.

Priya too had been having a recurring dream for almost twenty years and no one had listened to her either.

It finally came true.

So now you roughly know the background of these people. How I came into the picture is another story. Not to worry, for I am the story teller and will give you the entire details as we go along. I know you must be wondering how I arrived in Chandigarh.

CHAPTER 7

I was a bit restive for I had had a long day. It was 7.30 in the evening. Suddenly the phone rang. It was Gullu.

"*Jay*-deep! Gullu here! I hope you haven't forgotten me already." It was more of a statement than a question.

"No-*ooo*!" I tried to mimic him. "How can I? You labeled me a potential rapist." And we laughed.

"*Jay*-deep! Can you come over to my house right now? I know it is late, but why don't you come? I want you to meet someone special."

"No problem. But you will have to promise not to let me go home dehydrated. Because I was just about to start my anti-dehyration therapy!"

"*I* don't want to be dehydrated!" and we laughed some more. Marie had gone back to England since her school had re-opened after the vacations. I parked my car in his drive and as I got out of the car, a powerful light came on automatically. I was a bit surprised for I had never seen such lights in any Indian homes that I had visited. It was a new gadget which Gullu had brought from London. Gullu came to the door and gave me a friendly hug. I was to be at the receiving end of many such hugs from him.

"Wel-come, *Jay*-deep! What I mean to say is, well, come on inside! Why are we keeping the bottle waiting!!" His eyes crinkled again.

The lobby had a few chairs. It was understandable, for while Gullu was in England, only the caretaker Chandan Singh and his wife lived there. As I looked around, I was suddenly rooted to where I stood. The wall on the right side was adorned by a single black and white picture of the most beautiful woman I have ever seen. She was looking upwards. The side pose made her neck look as if it started from Ambala, a town 45 kilometers away, and ended somewhere behind the lake in Chandigarh or something like that. On closer scrutiny, it seemed to me like it was a swan's neck. Gullu was observing me as I stared at the photograph.

"Are you going to stand there forever, Jay-*deep!*? I need to know because the whisky is evaporating. Soon there will be nothing left and we shall have to get drunk on water or soda. Whatever!! The photograph that you are staring at belongs to my sister Vera. She is getting older by the minute, waiting to meet you!"

That brought me back very suddenly. He guided me into the drawing room. I froze again. Remember, in the Lord's year 1964, I was 15 and that is the time when I saw her for the first time in that movie. She was all of 23 years of age at that point of time. She was the heroine in the Indian war epic Haqeekat. My mind raced back and I could see her prancing down the hillside dressed in a hilly attire, straight into the arms of Major Bhadur Singh, our own Dharmender. Her large dove eyes seemed to penetrate the very soul of Major Bahadur Singh, searching for some after-the-war assurances. I can never forget the last scene of the movie where both of them are lying on the slopes of some mountain in Ladhakh, battered and bruised, bleeding from all over, their hands inching towards each other, grimacing in pain and effort. Just when their fingers are about to touch, their souls decide to abandon their bodies, only to unite forever, in a place where souls usually unite. I have always wondered at the stupidity of the director. Why couldn't he have let their fingers meet if they wanted to meet so desperately? Maybe their souls would have flown, hand in hand all the way to heaven. No, this man wanted mileage from death too.

After that movie, I made it a point to see every movie of hers. Heer Ranjha, Hanstey Zakham and many more. All of them had one thing in common. She either died a violent death or she burnt to death.

The funny part was that she was the author of all the stories in which died violently.

That day, when I was 52, she had to be 60. She was standing at the far end of the room. I stared at her, mesmerized, not being able to break eye contact. Here I was. In the same room with the first celebrity of my life and I was totally spell bound. It seemed to me that I had turned into the same 15 year old who became besotted by this beauty, 37 years ago. She was the same charming Priya, the same graceful Priya. She looked at me. It is obvious that she had been briefed about me. She was the proud owner of the most radiant smile if there was one. She continued to smile. I smiled back. There was a difference in the smiles though. Hers' was the friendly smile greeting a new friend. Mine was that of a zombie, a filler, not knowing what the next step should be. My heart raced at a pace it was not used to and definitely not after the stents had taken their exalted place in my coronary arteries, allowing blood to nourish thirsty areas of my cardiac muscle.

"*Jay*-deep! Don't act like a star-struck-kid. Here, she is only my kid sister! Vera, meet *Jay*-Deep. You will like him. He is not such a bad guy, never mind the way he looks and dresses." Gullu, it seems was on a perpetual high, his crow lines accentuated by his smile which seemed to be a permanent fixture on his face. *If his visage had been a golf course, we would get a free drop!*

I walked towards Priya in a trance like state.

"Hello Jaideep! Any friend of Gullu's is a friend of mine. You are most welcome." She spoke in a slow husky drawl. She proffered her tiny hand which disappeared in my large paw, in a firm handshake. I resolved never to wash my hand after that day. Thank God for small mercies for I did not crush her hand in my excitement. It was so soft and cold that I was surprised that it had not melted after I let it go. She retreated a few steps and said contemplatively, "Gullu, he doesn't look so funny to me and neither is his dress sense that bad." And she inspected me from top to bottom. The two of them laughed. Actually Gullu laughed and Vera giggled.

"I have been dreaming of this for many years. You want to pinch me or should I pinch you?" I stammered.

"Vera!" shouted an alarmed Gullu, "Don't let him touch you, Vera! You have no idea what these *Sar-dars* might do! He has already had a whiff of the booze! Be very careful because once a little of it goes inside his head there is no telling what he is capable of! Marie was ever so lucky that day!" Gullu shouts in mock horror. Vera, the actress that she was, responded with an expression of horror which seems very real. I am instantly alarmed. It seemed to me that I should run for my life.

But then Vera smiled and said, "In that case, I think *I* should be the one to pinch you, Jaideep."

The 'I' was very expansive. And she gave me the lightest pinch anyone could possibly give and looked for my reaction. I felt the beauty of it instantly and give out an exaggerated yell. She laughed. Gullu was thrilled for some reason. His wrinkles or whatever one calls the crow feet, were working overtime. Now I was sure that she was the same beautiful woman of the photograph in the lobby. She had changed. One has to, with age. She was naturally older. The skin was no longer what it used to be or what it is with makeup for a shot. The hair had a little red tinge because of the henna which she used. The smile was the same. She was wearing a cotton pastel shade churidar suit, which suited her well. Her long mane cascaded past her hips like a winter waterfall. A braid would not have looked so alluring. She flicked her hair as it fell over her face with her wrist ever so often because of her habit of talking with her head bent at an angle and her eyes looking up at the person she is talking to, just like the picture on the wall. She held a cigarette in her left hand while she talked to me.

She didn't inhale the smoke. She was not wearing lipstick or any mascara. She was a picture of simplicity. We talked about everything under the sun. She laughed a lot. So did I. I was at my happiest best.

"Jay-deep! You and Vera get along like a *house on fire*! But for God's sake, don't ignore me!"

I had no idea what that meant. English was a funny language. I had heard that phrase for the first time. Since he was smiling when he said it, I assumed that I had not put my foot in my mouth. So I just smiled my zombie smile.

Sometimes wearing a stupid smile on the face gets you out of a lot of sticky situations. Add a shrug of the shoulders to it and things get pretty much sealed.

Vera looked at me and smiled. There was a lot of smiling going on. I knew we would be great friends.

"Jaideep! I haven't laughed so much in a long time. Actually I am a very reserved person. I hardly know anyone in Chandigarh. People are different here. In Mumbai we have our own crowd. The people of Chandigarh have never seen a celebrity from close quarters. Mumbai's celebrities come in never ending waves, drowning the previous ones ruthlessly. Everyone knows that they are there only till the next wave comes in. We are just ordinary people for each other and not celebrities as we are here. Here, people don't know how to treat me. So I get flustered and don't know how to treat them."

"But that is the way I treat you too. You are the first celebrity of my life!" I said.

"Yes! But you are different now. You are not in awe of me any longer, or are you? You are Gullu's and Sam's friend. I don't mind being in your company at all. In fact you and Sam are so funny that I would love to see you both every day while I am in Chandigarh!"

Wow! I think. That certainly is a compliment. I was a court jester in the Queens' chamber. *Sam's understudy!* No, I am not being sarcastic. But I would love to be with her. She is very good with Urdu poetry and recites a lot of urdu couplets. This is another sphere among others where I am a total nincompoop. I have tried memorizing a few but they have failed me at the wrong moment. Or should I say right moment?

On another evening, I asked her about her acting. She informed me that she is basically a Shakespearian theatre actor.

"Just look at me. I was born in India and bred in England, where I joined theatre. From speaking accented Shakespearean English to speaking in Hindi which I can't speak at all, is a huge task. I could speak Urdu. But Hindi was another thing. When Chetan Sahib asked me for an audition for Haqeeqat, it was a nightmare for me."

I know that her dialogue delivery was very different. It was very slow, as she speaks in *real* life. It is almost a slow Texan drawl. But when she is up there on the screen, I don't think anyone is using their ears. It is only the eyes that are watching her.

I told her that I write.

"Which language?" she asked me, her eyes smiling. Obviously she had taken me for an amateur writer who writes middles in newspapers as a hobby.

"In English!" and she turned up her eyebrows.

"What do you write about?"

"I have just come out with my novel called *VINCULUM*. I am the author of India's first book on Golf, called *THE OTHER SIDE OF GOLF*. I have a letter from President George Bush, Sr. who wrote to me for that book." I tried to impress her.

"I would like to read your novel. I don't care about that silly game, golf. What is the novel about?"

"It is the story of 4 friends who join a medical college in Shimla and their journey through and out of it."

"Sorry, but I don't know what Vinculum means."

"I knew it. It means many things, but most of all it is the ligament which joins the carpel bones of the hand and the ligaments are called Vinculi. It also means a stepping stone or an isthmus. Here I have used it as a stepping stone or an isthmus which joins two phases of the lives of these four boys, adolescence and puberty, happiness and sorrow, dreams and reality and so on. It is what I call a facto-fiction."

I had brought a copy of the book along just in case the conversation veers towards the literary. I went to my car to fetch it. I presented it to her, bowing low.

"To the first celebrity who has herself asked to read my book." I said.

She immediately stood up and bowed in return, totally filmy style, and said, "Thank you, Jaideep. I must warn you that I am exceedingly lazy. I can't tell you really as to when I might actually get around to finishing it. But I promise I will do it."

I met her the next day. She informed me that she had finished the book. It took her a major part of the night to read it. I was thrilled and secretly very proud.

"Jaideep! It is a great book. Congratulations. I didn't think you could write so well. I counted thirty four T.V. episodes for the book. I don't delve in T.V. myself, but I will introduce you to someone who does."

She left for Mumbai after a few days. Gullu had to leave for England too. We had become good friends in those few days.

CHAPTER 8

A few days later, the phone rang in my clinic at 7 o'clock in the evening. It was Vera.

"Jaideep! I am here! Come!" that was all she said. The brevity had conveyed what had to be said and what was expected of me. I rushed to her house after telling my secretary to call me if there was any patient. There she was, as radiant in her smile as she ever was.

She had her arms spread wide and happily screamed, "Jaideeeep!"

It seemed to me that I was supposed to go across and give her a hug or get lost in hers. I am not too sure if I should do that to a celebrity. My hugging is limited to my male friends just to show solidarity. Our Indian style of showing friendship between the males is often misinterpreted by the Western world as a gay gesture. There is, I must warn you nothing gay about that gesture or me. So I walked up to her hesitantly and offered a handshake. She was stunned. Her expressions said all. Damn villager! Backward lout! Sam, who was a much travelled man, went up to her and gave her a hug. He joined his bearded cheek to her soft cheek on each side, puckering his lips without making actual contact with her cheek and produced the kissing sound, 'bvooch'!!! She reciprocated in a like manner. Now, that was the way sophisticated people greeted each other. I kicked myself for being so ignorant. Arshole, I call myself. I feel like one too for not being able to latch on to such fineries of social interaction.

Gullu pored chillies on my wound by chiding me, "*Jay*-deep, why didn't you give her a hug?" I think there was some salt too!

I shrugged my shoulders, totally embarrassed. I had nothing to say. Sam had been all over the world and had performed this greeting with élan many times to ladies in the golf club. I had observed this ritual but never have I thought that I too will meet sophisticated people one day who would expect me to join cheeks with them and produce the 'bvooch' sound!

Sam chipped in and said, "Vera, good to have you back."

"Yes! It feels nice to be back in Chandigarh when Gullu is here. So Sam! How have you been? And how is that lovely wife of yours?"

"Oh! She is quite an armful now!"

"Go on! She is such a petite little thing. You men are demons! Gullu, why don't you pour drinks for everyone?" and as she smiled, her eyes crinkled at the edges just like Gullu's.

Gullu did the honors with his man-Friday, Chanan Singh. He was the caretaker of the house and lived in the garage with his family. His wife Laxmi was a portly lady with a happy disposition. She was aware that Vera would now sit in the same chair for the next three hours hence the duty of looking after the guests would fall on her shoulders. Gullu was a happy drinker himself and he had come to know about the drinking habits of Sam and myself. I looked at Vera. She appeared to be sulking. Was she annoyed with me?

She hadn't addressed me directly even once.

"Vera, what do you do in Mumbai these days?" I asked as the disastrous greeting episode is drowned in the whiskey that we have imbibed.

"Oh! I don't have much to do these days really. I rarely get out of the house before 6 in the evening as I do in Chandigarh. Chetan Sahib doesn't keep too well these days, so I am with him mostly. I don't have too many friends. Life is generally very laid back." She replies and inhales a puff of the cigarette that she has in her left hand.

"These cigarettes are going to kill you slowly."

"Haan, haan! I am in no hurry to die either! Either people in Mumbai will get me killed or the cigarettes will kill me. I prefer the cigarettes."

"So if you know that people in Mumbai have bad intentions for you, why don't you shift to Chandigarh? This way you can die slowly with your cigarettes and us for company!"

"Jaideep! In Chandigarh I will not die because of cigarettes! I will die of pure boredom. That kind of slow death I don't want. I have nothing to do here. Apart from the two of you, I hardly know anyone in Chandigarh. And!" she adds expansively as if she is giving a dialogue for a movie, "neither do I care to know anyone else!"

"Chandigarh is a place where you can know everyone who think they matter, in just one evening. All you have to do is throw a party. Call those who you think are worth it and lo and behold! You know the whole town. No one in Chandigarh ever misses an invite! For them, the chance to be seen, meet people, have free booze and food is too much of a thing to miss."

"No! I think I will stick to Mumbai and die when my time comes. I don't think the boys can wait too long to do me in!" and she laughed sarcastically.

We talked about the occult, something in which we were both very interested. She told me about her mother who was clairvoyant. It seemed that she used to get dreams which came true. Vera told me that Gullu was clairvoyant too. She herself had been getting a dream for the last 20 years. I was intrigued. I did not know if Vera was also a clairvoyant.

Her visits to Chandigarh were frequent because of Gullu. Once, Chetan Anand, the director, came along with her. He wasn't doing very well. I even did a Holter E.C.G (24 hour ECG) on him. He died shortly after his visit to Chandigarh in Mumbai. I never did like him particularly because he had cheated Vera by putting her in a clause where she could never make movies with any other banner. She told me that most of the stories for his movies had been written by her. It seemed to me that she was obsessed with death. In quite a few of her movies she died violently. If they were all her doing, it wasn't a very healthy trend. She also told me that she didn't care too much for Chetan Sahib's younger brothers either. It seemed she had a special dislike for one of them, for she felt he was not a nice man to know. We argued on that because I was a great fan of the younger brother. I also sensed a certain depression creeping into her after Chetan Anand's death

CHAPTER 9

Anita Bansal and I were having coffee one day when she asked me if I would like to come for a meditation session. She had turned my reading habits on to a different tangent. She was the wife of a high ranking police official of Haryana. Many a time, I had been left wondering if he was really a Police official, because everything about him was furthest from my image of men in Khakhi. He was into spirituality, meditation, past life regression, hypnosis etc. He did not even raise his voice. Anita was the same. The first time she came to my clinic was as a patient; after that I became her disciple. Under her tutelage, from reading fiction, I started off on to Dr Brian Weiss, Paramhans Yogananda, James Redford, Rumi, and finally got into Reikhy.

I readily agreed. The meditation session was to be held by a Calgary based lady, Ruby Bedi, who turned out to be a self styled tantric also. She was a plump lady with a very sweet disposition. Anita Bansal introduced me to her after the meditation session. I paid a nominal charge of Rs 100 for the right to attend it and for the tea that we were served after the session. Retrospectively, I thought it is all humbug. But at that point of time I was very impressed with the lady for this was my first of many meditation sessions I was to have with her. Ruby had a mesmerizing voice and as she took us through the meditation, we were lulled into believing whatever she wanted us to believe. That day she attempted to take us into a past life regression. I did not quite remember what I went through. It seemed I was a lion or something in my past-life living in caves in some prehistoric era. A lion in a prehistoric era has neither any historic value nor any vital relationship to my journey through this world. A lion was just an animal gorging on other creatures, big and small. I finally made up my mind that past life regressions are all stupid hoaxes that people lump on unsuspecting fools like me.

We became friends. Ruby was on some sort of a mission and she joined an inter-religion peace movement that took her all over the country. She had plans to make a meditation center somewhere in Dehradun. She was perpetually travelling. It seemed that she was also collecting funds for her project. She told me of the saint who used to come to her house since she was a kid. He used a brick for a pillow. He had used the same brick for so long that there was a deep indentation in the shape of his head on the brick where he rested his head. Ruby insisted that her father's was the only household that the saint visited frequently.

One day, Ruby told us, he came visiting her house. She was nine years old then. He greeted her parents, Ruby and the servants. He sat with them for some time and then bade each member of the family farewell and left. Half an hour later, a servant came running to their house and informed Ruby's father that the saint was no more and that he had ended his earthy sojourn about four hours ago. Everyone was flabbergasted.

It seems that the saint had visited their house about three and a half hours after he died!

His age at that time was supposed to be 105.

She also told me that she could read a book without opening it. I immediately handed her a copy of my novel, Vinculum and asked her to tell me what it was all about. An expression of exasperation and anger clouded her face.

"Are you challenging me, Doctor Sahib? I suggest you don't do that" Her voice was so crisp and her tone so stern that the voice inside me started screaming at me to lay off. I did.

For once I listened to that voice and I said, "No problem! I believe you. It isn't important!" The only thing that I did not do was to urinate in my pants. If what people say about these tantrics is even half true, I didn't want to rub her on the wrong side. In fact I didn't want to rub her on any side. No, I didn't want to rub her at all. But another voice inside my head says, "See? She can't read the book without opening it and is just putting on a threatening act to scare you away."

Soon, Ruby had quite a following in Chandigarh. Soon, she was into satsangs (congregation of people singing religious songs) where her local fans collected and sang bhajans (religious songs). Days passed very quickly and one day she informed us that she was ready to leave for Calgary. Before she went, she wanted to have a big session in Chandigarh where her Guru would come from Delhi. We were curious to see what kind of man would be fit enough to be acknowledged by Ruby as her Guru. He looked a simple man with a perpetual condescending smile. He did not speak much. I too was introduced to him. They organized a bhajan session on a grand scale. I was not too interested in Bhajans. Ruby met my daughter and predicted her future. Not even one thing came true. We did not mind. No one was supposed to know everyone's future. But it felt nice to hear something good about your child's future. For those few moments, we were very happy and there was a feeling of security for her future. Ruby then left for Calgary with the promise of returning soon.

Ruby returned to India and turned up in the clinic one day accompanied by her friend Sunny. We had tea and during our small chit chat, I suddenly said, "Ruby, I have a very dear friend in Mumbai. I wonder if you could help her since she seems to be in some kind of trouble."

"What kind of trouble?" Ruby wanted to know.

"I don't know. To me it seems serious."

I told her about Vera. I told her about the name she used in the film world and her association with Chetan Anand. Surprisingly, both of them became very interested in the trip to Mumbai. Ruby looked at Sunny and they reached a decision that they should be in Mumbai the next day. I rang up Vera and told her about Ruby. Instead of being happy, Vera panicked, a reaction which I did not anticipate. She told me that she had no money to spend on guests.

"Jaideep, don't send anyone here. I don't have the money to look after them!"

It took a long time for me to convince her that there was no money involved. Then I told her that Ruby has certain powers related to the occult. That seemed to tilt the scales very quickly. Ruby and Sunny could have sensed an opportunity of being introduced into the world of Bollywood through Vera. Whatever the reason, they reached Vera's house the next day. Ruby told me later that Vera opened the door with a lot of trepidation.

The duo returned to Chandigarh after a few days. We met in my clinic again. I was very intrigued about things that transpired in Mumbai.

"Doctor Sahib! What a trip we had! We had to wait for some time after ringing the doorbell before she opened the door. I said hello and introduced myself. She was as lovely as you had told us. She did not invite us into the house straightaway. She had a scared look in her eyes. Suddenly her gaze fell on Sunny.

She shouted hysterically, "He is the one. He is the one who the faquir brought to my house in my dreams. I have been having this dream for twenty years and I have been searching for him. She animatedly asked Sunny, 'How old are you, boy?'

"It is my birthday today. I am 36 years old. Incidentally, the faquir wasn't wearing a black cloak. He was wearing a grey one." Sunny replied as if he was there when the faquir had offered the gift to Vera in her dreams.

After a moment of thought, Priya said, "Yes! Yes! He was wearing a grey cloak. It wasn't black! See, he remembers! He is that boy!"

Ruby continued, "I was just a spectator. As it is, it seemed that neither of them were even aware of my presence. I kept looking from one to the other wondering what was happening." She let out a little chuckle and then added, "Suddenly, Sunny broke into loud sobs. He was literally bawling like a child. I had never seen him behave in that manner before. Tears flowed down his cheeks as if the reservoir up there had burst. The next thing I know, both of them were hugging each other and crying, louder than before. Here I was, wondering if their best friend had died and someone had forgotten to tell me about it. I just stood around shuffling my feet like a nervous child. They stopped howling as suddenly as they had started as if they had run out of reasons to cry.

Finally we were invited in. Priya asked Sunny to sit next to him. We had dinner with her and then left for our hotel. It was very late. We met every day, visited temples and mausoleums along with her friend Moin. I think Priya was at her happiest best in those four days. I was very ill at ease when the time to depart arrived, for I was scared of a repeat performance from the two of them. All that did not happen. They just hugged each other for a long time, smiled and then we left peacefully."

All the while she was narrating this story, the hairs on the back of my neck were standing on their ends and a shiver was busy running up and down my spine. The

115

question whether she was able to help Priya sat just under the surface and I managed to keep it down only because I wanted to hear the rest of her story. I kept wondering if all this could be true? Could this happen in real life?

I couldn't stop myself any longer. In any case, Ruby's story had finished.

"Were you able to help my friend?" I asked Ruby impatiently.

"Doctor Sahib, there was nothing I could do to help her for I was reading the newspaper headline which said "PRIYA RAJVANSH DIES VIOLENT DEATH!" I can do nothing about it.

I was shocked. It felt as if a WWF wrestler had hit me on the good old chin. I felt my legs turning to jelly. I reminded myself that this is Ruby speaking. I can't disbelieve her, no matter how much I may want to.

"Did I ask you to help her out with her problems or did I ask you to get her killed? I seem to forget, which one was it?" my tone was sarcastic.

Ruby rarely got angry. She was very calm when she replied, "I know what you had asked me to do. But I can't help it. This is what I see written all over. I am sorry if I have hurt you. But Priya is not here for a long time. I can tell you that much!"

I was deeply perturbed. I am a qualified doctor. I am not supposed to believe in soothsayers of Ruby's ilk. But I just couldn't help but believing her. Looking at my mood, Ruby decided to leave. As I got busy with my patients, Priya receded into the deeper recesses of my brain. God has created a fantastic brain. It can conveniently forget what it wants to. With time, I didn't even remember Ruby's prediction.

Gullu returned to Chandigarh. This time Marie was with her. Our routine stayed the same. We invited everyone over to my house for dinner a couple of times. Vera addressed my maid by her first name, Laxmi who was tickled pink. She made it a point of seeing all her movies on the TV. We went to the golf club where a member drinking on the bar whistled loudly as he noticed her. Something of that kind has never happened in the Golf Club.

Vera was shocked. She said, "See! This can never happen in Mumbai. That is why I can never come and live in Chandigarh!" She couldn't get over it. I lodged a formal complaint with the President of the club. The member apologized to me at a later date. But the damage had been done. It was time for everyone to return to their bases.

Vera repeated her promise to me, "Jaideep! Come to Mumbai. I will introduce you to the film world. You can be their doctor. Also, I feel you are meant to be in that world. You are a creative man. You are wasted in Chandigarh."

"Not at this stage of my life, Priya! I can't leave Chandigarh. We are too deeply embedded in this city. I shall carry on writing here. Maybe a few best sellers will finally get me to Mumbai. But for the time being give me what I want most."

"And that is?"

"I want that black and white photograph of yours which is hanging in the lobby!"

"You can have that after I die. I will tell Gullu to give it to you after my death!" Gullu agreed. Matter over. I have no idea why everyone laughed so much even when death was being discussed. Is it because everyone wanted to ridicule the possibility of anyone dying despite knowing deep inside that the person was going to die and very soon?

Vera came to see me off at the gate. I suddenly asked her, "May I have the hug that I missed out that day?"

"I thought you will never ask" and she hugged me. That was the last hug I ever received from her.

Life went on conveniently till Gullu had a dream in London. He called up Priya and said, "Vera! I had another of my wretched dreams last night. Be very careful. I saw you being hit on the head with a club and then someone was throttling you with your dupatta (a part of ladies attire used to cover the upper torso). Your face was grotesquely bloated and you were dying in your toilet. Vera, please be careful."

Vera told her friends about her stupid brother getting another of his stupid dreams. Everyone had a good laugh. Why did they laugh? It was a very morbid dream. Did they laugh at the absurdity of dreams? The newspapers told us later that Chetan Anand's sons had hatched a conspiracy with their maid. The maid brought in someone from the south to help her in carrying out the murder. A night before she was to die, Vera, for some reason, panicked. Frantically, she called up Moin, her friend, to come to her house. It was late in the night. Moin was very reluctant for he stayed on the other side of Mumbai. It would cost him serious money to come on a taxi. Vera insisted that he came over. He did as she bade him. No one can deny her commands for long.

On his arrival, he found Vera tense. She told him, "Should you come to know tomorrow that I am dead, come to the house on the trot. All my gold ornaments and important papers will be in this hollow brass statue of Ganeshji. Take it with you and give it to my brothers when they arrive. Do you understand all that?" Moin promised to do all that and left.

Priya was supposed to go for a dinner to a friend's house the next night. She was wearing a thick gold chain amongst other ornaments. She was already late for the party. Priya being a very punctual person got the hosts worried. They rang her house to find out the reason for the lapse in punctuality. There was no answer to their rings. They went to her house to check. The house was not locked. Apparently, there was no one in the house. There was no sound. No one answered their calls. Then they found Vera lying on the toilet floor, quite dead of course. The bleeding was minimal. She had been hit on the head and then strangulated with her own dupatta. The gold chain has been used to drag her into the toilet for it had left deep marks on her neck. Her beautiful face was grotesquely swollen as predicted by Gullu.

Everything happened just as her brother had seen in his dream to the minutest detail.

The next day, Moin came to know of her death and did what Veera had asked him to do. I got the news from the newspaper in Chandigarh.

The headline was the same as predicted by Ruby.

It said "PRIYA RAJVANSH DIES VIOLENT DEATH"!

My family was shattered. I couldn't believe it despite the fact that Ruby had already predicted exactly the same headline. The news item described the murder with the entire gory details. I could not talk to Ruby for she was not in Chandigarh that day. I got a call from Calgary in Canada a few days later. It was Ruby. She wanted to know if I had heard about Priya. It seemed such a stupid question to me. Why would I not know? I asked her how she came to know about the murder.

"We were on our flight to Calgary and our plane developed a snag. We changed planes in Dubai. Sunny was very irritated. He picked up a newspaper lying in the aisle and angrily started flipping pages. I was in my seat with my eyes closed. I asked him to go back to page three and see what was written on the top right corner. There was the headline that I had seen and told you about. It said, "PRIYA RAJVANSH DIES VIOLENT DEATH."

I had no words left to say to Ruby so I put the phone down. My mind went back to what Ruby had told me during one of her last meetings before she left.

"Doctor Sahib! Remember. You will meet many people but a lot of them will leave you. Don't feel upset. They needed you for that time frame only. Once their need is over, they will move away."

I have remembered her words. I have met many people and befriended them and then over a period of time, they have moved on. I don't wonder 'why' any more. I have served their purpose or, they theirs.

The silver lining to the whole thing was that we heard that the perpetrators of the crime, the maid and her accomplice were all found guilty and sentenced. I had never met Ruby again. Maybe, I had fulfilled some need of hers too. I often met Marie and Gullu when they came to Chandigarh. There was a great change in Gullu. He played the songs that Vera loved again and again when we sat over drinks.

Every now and then he would heave a sigh and repeat the same dialogue, "*Jay*-deep, yeh sab kya ho gaya? Kaisey ho gaya?"(how did all this happen?) Initially, I would try to pep him up and try to console him about Vera. But with time and because of his repetitions, I

121

realized that he was asking the questions more out of habit and that whatever I might say, will have no effect on him. So I let him repeat the sentence over and over again. He was obviously going into depression. He started drinking all the time. It was beer or vodka in the mornings and whiskey in the evenings, though he was in denial all the time.

He lost a lot of weight as time passed by. To a person who met him for the first time, there was nothing obviously wrong with him.

His visits to England became more frequent and so did his trips to Mumbai. Vera's flat, her paintings and other effects had to be disposed of. His drinking went on despite being advised against it for he had developed a liver condition of unknown etiology. The combination of the liver disease, alcohol and the lack of will to live killed him within two years, pining for the sister he loved so much.

CHAPTER 10

I was sitting alone in the coffee parlor. The rest of my group was busy. Teji had an appointment for a wedding shoot. I was lucky, for my seat was vacant. I opened Tagore's book, Geetanjali, that I had bought recently. Geetanjali, a book of poems with a foreword by W.B. Keats! WOW! It is then that I realize what a handicap it is if one cannot read the original text because of lack of knowledge of that language.

A translation is like an almond from Afghanistan or California which has been artificially dehydrated and the oil sucked out. It just doesn't have the original taste.

Anyway, I don't know Bengali, so I tried to get as much out of it as I could by reading the translation.

Just then a threesome entered the coffee shop. They were busy jabbering in their native tongue. There were two very good looking girls. They did not seem to belong to Chandigarh. The moment they came inside, looking for their favorite ice cream flavor, they broke into English. One of them addressed the man behind the counter, "Bhaiyaaa (brother)! Can we have a taste of the Jaaamun?

The other one was more interested in the whiskey flavor. I was wondering what was in that man behind the counter that forced beautiful girls to break into accented English the moment they set eyes on him or whoever is on shift duty. Is it the effect of the ice cream? Or, is it that people think that only those who can speak the Queens' English will be entertained by the salesman? I have caught my wife speaking to the illiterate vegetable vendor who comes to our house asking, "How much for a kilo of Gobi?" (cauliflower) in English.

Anyway, I found the gentleman more interesting. He was sporting a huge moustache! I was reminded of my own. It also took me back to Zurich.

"Mr Singh! How do you get it up?" the burly Swiss security officer at the Zurich airport immigration counter had asked gruffly.

With a question like that, one has to be sure which aspect of mine is being allured to. Whenever one goes to any official counter or even a doctor's chamber for that matter, where one could be at the receiving end, one is rather cautious and overly well mannered.

So I had replied sheepishly, "Get what up, Sir?"

"I mean how do you get your mustache up, man?!" he thundered. A squeaky voice from a personality like his would have been grossly unfair. He himself sported an impressive moustache too, but it wasn't like mine.

We call the one that he has a 'walrus moustache'. It is bushy and it curves downwards because of it's weight and the owners' psychological makeup. In addition he owned an impressive looking gun which was very obviously and ominously staring at all and sundry.

Indians have something in common with the Turks in addition to our love of coffee. It is the moustache. Maharan Pratap had gone to war because of it, if you remember how the story goes.

Mine has been called the *'cornea tickler'*. On occasion it has also been called the *'windscreen wiper'*. It is rather large and bushy but unlike the Swiss guards' it also defies gravity with a fair amount of élan and at the same time, defiance. After so many years, it now seems a pedestrian issue, but the rising has never been easy. I have had to train it for many years. You might find it even funny, but since the age of 14, that is ever since soft hair started sprouting on my upper lip, I have been a witness to this ongoing event most closely on a daily basis and sometimes on an hourly basis. I have been single mindedly involved in its' future role as a gravity defying apparatus, which, later became synonymous with pride. I have spent long hours twirling it at the ends and then pressing them into my cheeks with my index fingers. The ignoramuses of the moustache-less world might think that I have put in so many hours laboring over studies that my fatigued neck refuses to hold my head up. Hence I have to use my elbows and my index fingers to prop it up. I am now convinced that my moustache has a life of its own for the rainy season would keep them moist forever and the humidity never helped. Thus it was a personal battle to keep them from collapsing, very crest fallen indeed. However, my life has never been easy with my moustache, weather notwithstanding, for it has also posed some grave problems for me too like the one with the Swiss guy and then the Nigerian custom officer later.

When the Swiss guy posed that particular question, the year was 1984. I had completed a two year contract with the Government of Kwara State in Nigeria. It seemed to me that the political environment and conditions generally were not conducive for renewing my contract. The Nigerians, nay, for that matter the whole of Africa, has always been very unstable politically. The aspiring President had made too many noises against expatriates. Just the other day, we heard of a bus belonging to an Indian School in Lagos, the capital of Nigeria at that point of time, being burnt. The burning of a bus was not the real problem. The real problem was that the bus was full of Indian children. The driver of the bus, also a Nigerian, turned out to be a hero. He managed to save all them. That incident pre-empted any thought of my staying on in Nigeria. I decided to go back to India instead.

That is how I landed in Zurich. My itinerary included a night halt in Zurich. Those were the days of the so called Sikh extremism. I needed a transit visa for my family. The other problem was that the Swiss immigration officer in question was a large man, as I have already told you and who was flaunting a gun and a walrus moustache. It seemed to me that in recent years, people had changed their perception of me generally. Earlier, except for my family, a few friends, my patients and my golf four ball, I didn't exist for anyone in the world. It seemed to me that most people just happen to look through me as I if am made out of the finest glass that ever was. There are some who bestow a glance towards me only because of my garrulous turbans, for I am the proud owner of the snazziest collection of printed turbans this side and that side of the Suez Canal. A Sikh's identity is basically through his turban, beard and of course the moustache. Yes! I am a proud Sikh for I possess all three of them.

So why was the Swiss guard staring at me?

This guy, it seemed to me at the outset, had a problem with me, for he did not even cast a cursory glance at our passports. It was something that I thought was basic for an immigration officer to be doing. On the contrary, he acted as if he was a face or an aura reader. All that he did was to stare at me. I feared the worst. I imagined myself in the interrogation center, naked, without my turban, my unshorn hair going helter skelter, and undergoing third degree torture with the Swiss peeping into apertures, the existence of which even I never knew nothing about. I was sweating despite the air conditioning.

My brain was still working. I deftly put my three year old son's passport on the top of the pile but I soon realized that this action would be productive only if the man was interested in passports in the first place. It was so obvious to me that the man wasn't even vaguely interested in them. Suddenly, it seemed he had enough of my face because he opened his mouth for the first time. That is when he asked me the fatal question.

"How do you get it up?"

No one should ask a complete stranger this question.

I was zapped. I was also hugely relieved, for my apertures were seemingly safe from peeping toms for the time being. Also, all my unknown ones would continue to remain a mystery for mankind. That day at the airport, when the Swiss immigration officer mentioned my moustache, I heaved a sigh of relief and told him, "Oh! In India we have developed special manure for the moustache. We sprinkle it on the moustache and it grows like a wild bush! Then with a bit of love and grooming, off it heads skywards like the branches of a tree!" I felt as if I was a poet.

Thank God for the officer's sense of humor. The hall reverberated with his laughter and he quickly stamped our passports and we were through as tourists and not as terrorists!

I have undergone hardships because of my moustache once before in Lagos. Hence this was nothing new to me. In my humble opinion, Nigerians are as corrupt as Indians, if not more. There could easily be a tie between them. On a more personal level, the Nigerian people are unforgettable once you have interacted with them. Agreed, they are a violent race. But then, if you look around, which human race isn't violent? Given a chance, no one would like to be left behind. But one could easily fall in love with them too.

The Nigerians are very friendly people. They greet each other at every available oppurtunity, the length of which is usually directly proportionate to the importance of the person being greeted. Greetings are very important to them. The greetings routinely include queries about the health of the parents, children, the house, the farm, the goats, the yam, their beloved Peugeot 504 car, and anything else that would matter to the other. They are interspersed with sounds like 'eehha', 'ah-haaan!' or a loud 'ooh'. If the greeting is not behooving their social status, it would automatically means a loss of face and they take great umbrage to that fact. They have no permanent emotional bonding with their given religion or their politics. They could be Christians on a given day and then switch to being Muslims the next day. They could be members of any political party on one day and change the next. They will give their life for their most recent switch-over and will also take lives for them. And, if I may add, that could translate into many lives.

I, like every expatriate, needed a work permit if I had to work in Nigeria and for that I had to travel a long distance to and inside Lagos to reach the immigration office. The moustache welding immigration officer, greeted me profusely. He was most courteous and offered me a seat. He wanted to know when I arrived in Nigeria; if that was my first time in his country; whether Nigeria was treating me well. He wanted to know how he could be a help to me. I was most impressed. Suddenly, his tone changed.

"Mr Singh! You know that you cannot work in Nigeria if I don't give you the work permit?" he announced in front of the entire office staff.

"Yes, I know!" I acknowledged.

"So what do you have for me?" he raised his left eyebrow.

"I have just come into Nigeria. I haven't received my salary yet. I will give you when I get paid." I said with all the pathos I could muster in my voice.

Nothing seemed to move him. His eyes settled on my moustache. I was now scared.

"If you teach me how to get my moustache to go up instead of down like mine does, I will give you a work permit to work in Nigeria!"

I pleaded with him that it is because of the 'Fixo' that my moustache can do what his can't.

"Ah-haan!" he says, "Mistah Singh! Get me that concoction, whatever it is that you call it!"

There was an instant stalemate. No permit till I gave him the secret concoction that makes my moustache defy gravity. It seemed to me that I would have to go back all the way to Illorin, about 250 kilometers away from Lagos to fetch the concoction we call 'Fixo'! 250 kilometers in Germany on the autobahn is very different from 250 kilometers on a Nigerian highway.

Even a woman selling papayas on any Nigerian highway will wish you a safe journey.

It does give you an eerie feeling as if one is about to enter a war zone. I had brought a limited supply of the

Fixo. I have to make it stretch to a minimum of two years till I go back to India on leave.

I did all that because I had to work in Nigeria, didn't I? Wonder of wonders, after I parted with some of my precious 'Fixo', he even forfeited his customary bribe money, which is his Nigerian birth right. A Nigerian, they say will not even sneeze till someone 'dashes' him a bribe. A salesgirl will refuse to serve a customer till she gets some money. Today things might have changed though. In the anticipated excitement of finally achieving a skyward destined moustache, he quickly signed my papers. Two years later, I met him in Illorin, the capital of Kwara State, as I was coming out of a supermarket. He recognized me instantly. So did I.

"Hello Sah!" I said "I notice your moustache is still not up!"

"Ah! Doctoh!" he laughed out loudly, "you cheated me! You never told me how to use the liquid that you gave me!" and we hugged each other as if we were great friends. In fact we were. We are from the rare breed of males for whom the vegetation on our upper lips is a matter of life and death.

As I am thinking about this, the guy who has been searching for the ideal ice cream to devour in the company of the lovely ladies had already decided and left.

CHAPTER 11

It was past 7 p.m. A very grueling session of medical examinations of aspiring Merchant Navy Officers was over. At that odd hour, I didn't think it right to invite any of my friends over for coffee. I am of the reserved opinion that once in every while, one should enjoy solitude. So I went alone.

You see, there is a vast difference between loneliness and aloneness. Loneliness hurts but aloneness is something that helps you become a complete human being and can help you reach the top.

The moment I got out of my Toyota Inova, a reflex expletive gushes forth. The reason was that I had seen someone sitting in 'my' chair in Gelato. That was the first thing that I always noticed as I got out of my car. I definitely did not like that to happen. It isn't that the chair was mine. It was just a matter of habit. I have gotten used to sitting in that chair. People who pass by Gelato are also used to seeing me sitting there. And then there were those who think that since I was always there, I must be the proprietor.

There was a lady occupying the chair. She looked up as I entered.

"Hello, Sir!" she smiled happily.

There I go again. 'Who was she', I wondered. Is she a friend's daughter or a patient? I have deep worry lines on my forehead. They are like the S.Y.L. canal tributaries.

I said, "Hello to you too!"

She immediately got up and moved to another table. I was perplexed and before I could say anything, she said, "I know this is your seat."

"No, no! It is not my seat. Please don't get up."

"No, Sir! I know you always sit here." Now, I was zapped. How does she know?

"Have we met before?" I asked.

"Yes! I was here with my husband the other day and I told you that you look like a teacher who used to teach me Punjabi in college!"

"Ah! Now I remember" I lie. I take great umbrage to her reference to me as her look-alike Punjabi teacher. Punjabi teacher, my foot! For god's sake, couldn't she have said, 'My French teacher' or 'my Russian teacher' or anything else? Punjabi teacher sounds so corny and paendu (villager) type. But the damage had already been done. I deny any link to my mother tongue Punjabi, at least as a teacher of it.

"Sikhs do look alike, yes?" I probed her brain, "So what are you doing here all alone? I hope the coffee bug hasn't bitten you too?"

"No! My son is in the neighborhood for a birthday party. I had some free time to wile away so I decided to have coffee."

She looked a simple kind of lady to me. I guessed her to be about 30 years old. So I enquired about her husband who turned out to be in the wholesale footwear business. He and his brothers were in a joint family venture with their father. They lived in the same house with their parents. Her mother-in-law seemed to be some sort of a Jew who had no idea of what spending money meant. Maybe, she didn't even know that money was meant to be spent. Her elder sister-in-law is also a clone of the usual run of the mill tyrants!

Somewhere during our conversation, she dived into her purse and fished out a contraption which she says is used to take the extra layer of skin from the soles of her feet. It cost her 60 rupees.

"It cost me 60 rupees. My mother-in-law is going to ask me where I got the money for it. So I will hide it from her."

I was very surprised. Naturally! I mean if they have a good business going, they should be loaded. What would 60 bucks mean to their bank accounts? The coffee that she was having would cost her 63 bucks.

"I don't believe this. So if she is fussy about your spending 60 bucks, tell her you got this for 20. That will silence her!"

"She will say, 'get one for me too'. Then what do I tell her?"

"Then, after a few days, tell her you picked it up from a guy selling stuff on the pavement. You can't find him again."

That set her thinking and she said "hmmm . . . ."

"I can't even read a newspaper at home. My sister-in-law takes it away and I can't get to read it for she does not bring it back into circulation."

"So order your own newspaper, silly!'

"You would think my mother-in-law would let me waste another 60 rupees?"

"What is this thing your family has about 60 bucks? I think you yourself are too much of a sissy."

"A sissy is better than an outcast. If she came to know that I am having coffee here in Gelato, she will get a royal fit"

"What is your educational level and from where?" I don't know why but I just had to know.

"I am a Bachelor of Computer Sciences from a college in Landran on the outskirts of Chandigarh."

"So you can help the family business then."

"The family rules say that the women of the house have nothing to do with the family business!" Then she came out with the punch line that I had been waiting for. I have no idea why anyone should open their book of life to a complete stranger. That too, to someone who has a remote resemblance to your erstwhile Punjabi teacher! I think it is the coffee that does it. Or is it that people wanted to make friends with me at this stage of my life, especially the younger brood.

"Doctor, I am fed up. I don't know if I should carry on living this life because I am so bored. I am very depressed and I don't know what to do."

I did not want to open my ears to a long sob story. I had come for my coffee in solitude.

"Read my book, "Please Mom! It's my life!"

"I will. Where may I pick up a copy from?"

"It is available in all the major book shops in sector 17."

"O.K!" she said and then added that it was time for her to pick her son from the party and left.

I sat back and wondered at the kind of people who exist in this world. If this lady had to explain why she had the temerity to spend 60 bucks of the family kitty on a necessity, then what is the use of earning so much of money in the first place? I finished my coffee and since I have not seen her paying at the counter, I offered to pay for her coffee. The man on the counter told me that she has already paid for her coffee in advance.

I left the shop but my mind was in turmoil. Why? It is not my problem. I wondered why she had decided to tell me about her problem in the first place. What is it about me that made her spill the whole bag of worms? Is it my face?

CHAPTER 12

Anne Cherian and Jaspreet Nijjer are two Correspondents from the Times of India group. I had known them for some time now. I had gone to Gelato for a cup of coffee. They were already there. I asked them what new had happened in town in the last 24 hours. Just then, Vidhu Verma walked in. He sat in the chair which faced the ice cream refrigerator. There was a problem with the cooling system and a young man was on the job of repairing it. As soon as Vidhu made himself comfortable, he was spotted by the electrician. He immediately took out his mobile and it was fairly obvious that he had gone on the internet and taken out Shikar Dhawan's picture. He took about three minutes to stare at Vidhu and another two to stare at the picture on his mobile. The diagnosis was clear. Shikhar Dhawan was sitting in the coffee parlor with his friends. We were all looking at his reactions.

"He is who you think he is, but you can't take his picture." I said.

"But why?" he asked.

"Because it is in the contract that he has signed with Sahara."

He just could not take his eyes off Vidhu. Finally, it was as if half heartedly, he left. After about five minutes, he came rushing in and stood before me with his folded hands.

"Sir! There is a genuine request."

"And that is?"

"Can I please have a picture with Sir?" and he shook his head towards Vidhu.

We were all trying to control our laughter.

"Alright, but don't tell anyone, O.K.?" I said.

"Never, Sir!" Thus, it transpired that Vidhu became a local hero. Other people came to know about him because that youngster must have told at least a hundred people. Vidhu had to pose with others as well, till one day, people saw Shikhar batting in Mumbai on TV while Vidhu was busy drinking coffee in Gelato! Well, we had to apologize to some people, saying it was a joke.

Anne, who was the more talkative of two, was from Kerala, belonging to an Orthodox Christian sect. We called all people from the belt of Kerala, Tamil Nadu and Chennai, Malus, as they called everyone from regions north of New Delhi, Punjabis. They married very strictly into their own sect so that narrowed the chances of getting a good groom. She was on the plumpish side and looking at her palate desires, I doubted that she would ever lose the 5 kilos that needed to be lost. She had deep dimples in her cheeks which meant that she would get married and would be the apple of her mother-in-law's eye! At least that is what people in the Punjab believe.

"We met the most awesome person today. We went to the annual meet of an organization and there was this guy, must be like 6 feet 3 inches, huge man wearing a white kurta and pyjama along with a Gandhi topi. In total contrast to his dress, was his complexion, which was absolutely dark. But he wasn't a Malu. He was from Maharashtra. It turned out that he was the Chief Guest for the function! When he stood up to talk, I found him to be the most articulate speaker that I had the good fortune of hearing. His accent wasn't British, but what he had to say was in flawless language. What did you think of him, Jaspreet?"

"I totally agree. He was the Managing Director of the Dubba Wala Association of Mumbai. It is a co-operative society and has 5,000 Dubba-Wallas but overall, there are 40,000 men and women associated with them. Each member earns between 10 and 15 thousand rupees every month. Their job is to deliver 2,00,000 tiffen boxes to members daily and only once have they failed to deliver because of a bund (strike). Every Tiffin or Dubba or lunch box is picked up from the residence of the person and then delivered to his place of work at precisely the same time every working day of the year. The whole system works on the color coding and the code number of the area, which is painted on the Dubba! The fee depends upon the size of the tiffen and the area it has to be delivered to."

Anne was bubbling with enthusiasm, "They have to wear the white dress and the Gandhi topi (cap made out of cloth). It is the hallmark of the organization and anyone who fails to wear it, has to pay a fine of 200 rupees. An absentee has to provide a substitute, failing which he is fined 2000 rupees. So finely tuned is the functioning of the Dubba-Wallahs that Prince Charles on his trip to Mumbai had specially asked to meet with them. Since their routine cannot be disrupted, they offered to meet him at a particular railway station, to which the Prince acquiesced. Later, about 500 of them collected money and decided to send a 9 yard silk sari (the long cloth that Indian women drape around themselves) for Lady Camilla when the Price of Wales would finally marry the Lady. They also wanted to send her green bangles as a good omen."

Suddenly, Anne looked at her watch and let out a tiny shriek, which, because of tininess, failed to scare me, "Jaspreet, look at the time! Rahul is going to slaughter us! But first he is going to make mince meat out of us!!!" and they hurriedly picked up their mobile phones, purses and were out of the place before I could blink. That left me alone. I had not even ordered coffee yet.

The fellow who makes coffee for us was sitting under the Peepal tree. I had to signal to him to come and make me some strong coffee. He got up half heartedly, not wanting to leave the warm sunshine. I stretched my legs. If only the chairs were a wee bit more comfortable, I would probably sit for a longer time. Nevertheless, once I was ensconced in that chair, it felt as if I had come home. I did not want any of my friends to come and give me company. I had enough on my mind.

Just then, the door opened and two young sad looking girls came in as they were not sure of themselves and whether this was the right place to have coffee. One had elements of annoyance and arrogance attached to her sadness. The other one just looked sad. She went to the refrigerator and looked at the various choices of available ice creams. She wanted to taste some and finally settled on some chocolate flavor. Just for future reference I will call the two girls Dark Sad and Angry Sad.

Dark Sad looked at her friend and asked what she would like to have. Angry Sad was the taller of the two and thinner. She looked as if she had forgotten her waist at home. Dark Sad was a little darker and plumber. The thin one raised her head as if her head was too heavy to lift. It required a machine of some kind to help her out. She finally completed the job by raising her eyeballs herself. It seemed the eyeballs sent out a jet of some alien gas which almost floored Dark Sad. With that her eyeballs slowly, very slowly, descended down to the table level and her chin fell back into her cupped hand. Angry Sad then lifted her eyeballs and fried Dark Sad with her look.

"Don't you know that I always have coffee? *Cold coffee?*" she hissed.

Dark sad got up obediently and ordered a cold coffee for her friend. On returning, she attempted some dialogue which sadly stayed a monologue. She talked some more and then some more. Angry sad was in no mood to answer her. My coffee arrived in the meantime.

The two of them kept having their ice cream and cold coffee respectively, in a dark and deafening silence. Dark Sad's ice cream melted under the glares of Angry Sad while the cold coffee of Angry Sad became placid coffee for she did not even take a sip of it. It wasn't her loss for Dark Sad had paid for it. Suddenly, as if by co—incidence, Angry Sad's eyes focused on her coffee and she slurped it down. She got up, de-creased her dress top, pushed ten fingers through her hair and after a toss to the head, headed off towards the door. Dark Sad has not yet finished her ice cream so she picked it up and headed after her friend. Friend? Is this the way friends treat each other, even if they are annoyed over some issue?

A few days later I was again in my chair, very alone, at the Gelato coffee parlor, sipping coffee and reading that day's issue of Hindustan Times. In walked Dark Sad and Angry Sad. It was absolutely déjà vou. It was as if I was reliving the same scenario. Angry Sad was as angry and Dark Sad was as sad. The only difference was that Dark Sad was trying harder to please Angry Sad and that too very unsuccessfully. As Dark Sad sat down with her cold coffee with ice cream and concentrated hard on scooping the ice cream out of her coffee, Angry Sad started giving her the same glares. The glares bounced off Dark Sad because she did not know about the glares. Meanwhile, Angry Sad seemed to be getting angrier and her glares seemed also to be getting hotter by the minute. Don't forget for an instant that I am the same silent spectator, observing all and sundry with as much interest as I did on the previous occasion. I might as well tell you that I am a compulsive interferer. There is a voice inside me which was screaming away to glory, "Doc! Don't do it!" again and again. I am a good guy. I listened to the voice for a long time but the voice knew when it was on the losing side. Suddenly, I burst out, "Excuse me!"

Since the third table was unoccupied and there was no one else sitting in the parlor excepting the guy on the money machine, Angry Sad and Dark Sad looked up. I caught their eyes simultaneously. It was indeed a tough ask. It seemed that there were all possibilities of my developing a squint.

"I know this is terribly bad mannered of me, but I have seen the two of you here before."

If *I* had been told that, my answer would have been a curt, "So?"

But Angry Sad and Dark Sad were good girls. It was Angry Sad who replied, "Yes, Sir! We have also seen you sitting here. Incidentally that is my chair that you are sitting on."

I was taken totally unawares. I knew for a fact that it was my chair. Now it seemed that Angry Sad is the real owner of that chair. Nevertheless, I was in no mood to make small talk about ownership of chairs. I had a completely different agenda.

"May I be completely truthful with you and come to the point?"

"Yes." it was Angry Sad again.

I looked at her in the eye and said "I am a doctor and a writer. This means that my power of observation is a little sharper than most others. I noticed that when you two came in last time, you were very angry. Correct?"

"Yes!"

"And that too for no special reason at all?"

"Yes."

"And your friend here was trying very hard to placate you?"

"Yes."

"And you did not relent?"

"Yes."

"And today, you are doing the same?"

"Yes."

"You have been glaring at her for some mysterious reason?"

"Yes! You are very observant."

"No! Even a blind man would have noticed!" I looked at Dark Sad and asked her "Were you aware that she was bestowing upon you a certain angry look at you continuously?"

"No!" she replied.

"May I ask you why you are behaving like a door mat? Why are you tolerating such terrible behavior time and time again?"

"No, she is such a pooch. I love her. She can never be angry with me. She is a bit tired." And her right arm lanced out and she pulled Angry Sad's left cheek. Angry Sad suddenly smiled. She was no longer angry. Dark Sad was no longer sad. They both smiled at me.

"We are here for our MBA. We have just come back from a project and were trying to relax."

"Funny way to relax, I must say." I said with a smile hovering on the border of my lips. They seemed to understand.

"I just tease her all the time. She also knows. Ask her." said Angry sad.

"Yes, Sir! She teases me a lot. I understand her so well. She is such a wonderful person that I don't mind it at all. I accept whatever she does." And she pulled No-longer-Angry-Sad's chin. No-longer-Angry-Sad smiled. She had a very lovely smile. I agree with Dark Sad that she is a wonderful person.

"Sir! You say you are a writer. What kind of books do you write?"

"I write on social subjects. I even have a novel and two on golf. In fact I write on every subject excepting Medicine!"

"Why?"

"Even you can write a book on medicine. All that you have to do is to take 10 books and plagiarize them. Voila! You have a book. But if you have to write on a social theme book or a novel, you have to use your own brains. I like picking my own brains. Who knows, one day I might even write a book in which the two of you are a part!"

Still-Dark-but-not-so-Sad-now and Not-so-Angry-nor-Sad smiled at me.

I met them again after a few days. Was-Angry-and-Sad was sitting in my chair, happily talking to Dark-who-too-is-not-sad-anymore. She immediately got up and offered 'my' chair to me. I very decently declined the offer. They were ecstatic about the fact that they were off to Delhi for their internship. They were hoping to see me after three months, in the same chair and at the same time. I say, "Inshah-Allah!"

"What will happen to your boyfriends?"

"Boyfriends?!" and they looked at each other and laughed.

"Boy *frieeends*! As In 'boyfriends'! Every girl seems to have boyfriends these days," I said making the quote-unquote sign with my fingers, "some even have more than one!"

"No, Sir! We don't have boyfriends. We simply don't have the time for all that presently. We don't have the inclination either."

I looked at them and smiled. I have been bumping into them on and off. They are no longer angry sad and dark sad. They are just happy people. They have finished their studies and are doing their internship in some Corporate in Delhi.

CHAPTER 13

Ajit Pal Walia called, "Sir, where are you? Are you at the clinic or somewhere else?"

"I am at the Clinic." I replied.

"Busy or are you free for coffee? I am in the area and can come in two minutes."

"Come, come! We will have coffee."

"At Gelato?"

"Yes."

Ajit is a young aggressive lad of thirty. He dealt in books. In fact he is a distributor of some good books from national and international publishers. I have no idea how he gives them cheaper than the marked prices. Normally, people sell them at the prices mentioned on the books. He supplied books to mainly schools, institutions and libraries. He had a very smart and good looking assistant and after a point of time, their combined literary interests made them decide that they should increase the field of their interests. So they married. His wife belonged to a Punjabi family which decided to convert to Christianity. So now they were Christians and they talked about Christ and His goodness at every opportunity. Ajit is duty bound to become a faithful too. Although he is a turban sporting Sikh and has a beard, he goes to church, maybe on

Sundays. He did not talk much about his new religion though.

As we sat and chatted about books, publishers and the art of selling books, he recieved a call from Gaurav, an employee of Ajit Pal. He has a different policy on hiring people. Instead of full pay, he gives them conveyance and petrol allowance, food and lodging when they go out of town and a percentage of what they sell. This way, they make more money and have an incentive to work harder.

Ajit Pal told Gaurav that since we were in Gelato, he should come and meet him there. He informed me that Gaurav belonged to a joint family and that they stayed in Banur, about two hours away from Chandigarh. He did an 'up-down' everyday. Gaurav is a very happy-go-lucky boy who was not on the lookout for a bride yet. So he had a lot of time on his hands and wanted to do well in his job. It seemed to me that Ajit Pal is quite fond of him. I soon discovered why. The door opened and Gaurav walked in. His eyes lit up the moment he saw me. I could have sworn that I have never seen him before. Apparently, he had. He gave me an ear to ear grin and bent down to touch my feet for my blessings. I am not embarrassed by that gesture these days, for a lot of young people do that to me. Moreover, if at this ripe age, I shirk to bless someone who has touched my feet. It just means that I don't consider myself fit enough to bless anyone.

"Sir! My life is made. First I get to read your book. Then I get to meet you!"

I was secretly thrilled. I blessed him and asked him how he got my book.

"Sir! I sell your books too! Normally I don't read the books that I sell but I read yours. It is a great book!"

He suddenly remembered that he had come to meet his boss and finally decided to acknowledge him.

After being briefed about what he was supposed to do the next day, he left, but not before touching my feet again.

"He is a very good worker. I bought him the bike and the E.M.I.s are taken out of his salary. He lives almost eighty kilometers away."

I looked at my watch. It was already seven p.m. and getting darker by the minute.

"He does this every day on the highway?"

"Yes." For some reason I was worried.

We shifted to other topics. The new publisher whom Ajit had introduced me to was a very well read and spiritually inclined person. I am amazed at the words in his spiritual vocabulary. I am not sure if he himself believed in all that he was saying because if one has to do all that he said there is to do, then one is already in the nirvanic state of mind. I was not so sure if he had reached that level yet. Such people are interesting to listen to in short spurts. That way they kept invigorating the discussion. We discussed the book *AUTOBIOGRAPHY OF A YOGI* by Paramhans Yoga Nanda. He had read most of these books. I told him about Yogteshwar Giri who was Swami Paramhans Yogananda's guru. The two would meet in Los Angles while he was in Calcutta! A simple case of transporting his body through space! He went into a meditational state and gave up his life which was also emulated by Swami Paramhans in Los Angles in front of an audience of 10,000 people. The publisher in turn told me that he knew Yogeteshwar Giri's younger brother very well. The topic shifted to levitation which some Gurus delve in and he informed me that he had been to Tibet and met a Lama who could levitate. In fact he could fly from one place to the other. He would put all his weight on the right big toe and then propel himself around.

"I asked him if I could do the same thing. The Lama said that I could, if I practiced enough." He says.

I looked at our friend and wondered if he was pulling my leg. But he was a picture of seriousness. The Chinese movies that one sees have the hero and villain fly around forests and we think they are flying around because of wires and ropes. Is it possible that the monks had learnt the art of levitation to that extent?

Walia had recently rented new premises in the Industrial Area. The area was huge as compared to what he had earlier. At least now his books were decently displayed. People could come and read and order books at leisure. Still, the number of books that he had in his stock was so huge that one can't help but wonder how he used to manage them earlier.

We discussed ways and means to increase the sales of my book *PLEASE MOM! ITS' MY LIFE*. He also wanted me to get the new publisher to translate the book into Hindi and Punjabi. It has already been translated into Spanish and Marathi. I had recently received a friend request on Facebook from a person called Eduardo. He lives in Mexico. Eduardo told me that for some reason, he wanted to kill himself and then he got to read my book. He decided not to die and now he is a changed man. I was thrilled. I am like that. I get thrilled on such things very easily.

We got up to leave. Arjun was waiting for me. I asked him if he wanted anything.

"I want to eat food." he said.

I gave him a 10 rupee note, which somehow disappeared in a bizarre Houdini act. I don't mind. I remembered that it was our responsibility as normal humans to take care of people like Arjun. Come to think of it, if all well to do Indians gave the poor what they needed, there would be no needy left. Right? Wrong! These people were used to begging, and even if we provided sufficient money for their daily needs, they will still fail to sustain themselves. The begging would still carry on and in any case, most of the beggars were a part of a syndicate which was worth crores of rupees. The people who ran these beggars would not let them out of their clutches. I wasn't so sure if Arjun was not a part of the begging syndicate. I wondered if he was born the way he was or did the syndicate break his legs when he was a toddler and then inducted him into the profession? In all probability, he had to share his 'earning' with them. I didn't stick around to see if he had gone to satisfy his hunger or would he still be sitting there looking for some more suckers susceptible to emotional blackmail.

After some time, Arjun was conspicuous by his absence. Driving past St. Carmel School, I noticed him sitting at the red light crossing, his hair in different shades of brown and he had used gel to perm them up. He looked different. I greeted him and he gave me a smile. After many months, I saw him again, but this time he was on the Madhya Marg, driving a tri-cycle specially made for handicapped people. He looked older. I wondered who the good Samaritan was who had bought him that contraption.

Anyway, his place in front of Gelato ice cream parlor has been taken over by an old man who is covered by a ragged blanket and I noticed that quite a few of those coming out of the bakery dropped a 10 rupee note in his lap. Teji was doing a money count. After some time, he got bored.

"This is too much yaar! In half an hour he has collected 80 rupees without even having to ask for anything!"

CHAPTER 14

I wanted to ask Ajit Walia something more about the publisher he had introduced me to the other day. But he was unavailable on the phone for a long time. When I finally managed to speak to him, his voice sounded as if he was in deep pain. I wondered why. I did not ask him the reason. He told me that he was busy at someone's funeral and would be free only after an hour or two. I wondered who had decided to leave us.

I called up Inderpreet to join me for a cup of coffee. We sat there for the larger part of an hour. He was in the Insurance Business. He also had some interest in the real estate business. It seemed to me that the real estate people would soon take over all the available land in the country. These days, everyone seemed to be interested in making money. The price of land had been artificially increased and as a result, farmers in Punjab, big or small, had sold off their land and come into huge amounts of money. Most of them acquired S.U.V.s, Audis, Volvos and Mercedes cars. They still had so much money left over that they splurged as never before. Many of them exhausted their money quickly. They had thus lost their land and their money and were left with cars.

Inderpreet wanted me to invest in the IREO properties. I had no knowledge about these things. I told him that I need to leave some money for my wife in case I cop it one of these days.

"You are very right. See what happened recently to my father. We ended up spending 27 lakhs for his illness. Each injection was worth one lakh. If we did not have money kept aside for such emergencies, we would have been finished. Out of your savings, you should keep at least 30 percent of your savings for your wife. 30% should be kept for your own self, 30 percent for medical expenses and 10 percent should be kept to play around with in the form of investments and property." I decided to keep that in mind.

The phone rang again. It was Walia on the line.

"Where are you, Sir?"

"I am having coffee with Inderpreet. Come join us."

He walked in after a short while and sat in the third chair.

"Whose funeral were you attending?" I asked.

"An employee of mine died. I had to go to Banur." He said sadly.

"Banur? Doesn't Gaurav live in Banur?"

"Yes. You know Gaurav?" He seemed to have forgotten that I met him in Gelato a few days back.

"He is the jolly fellow whom we met here a few days back. You told me that you had bought him a bike. He had touched my feet and was praising my book? Wasn't he Gaurav?"

"Yes! He died yesterday! He was going home for a function he had arranged for his mother who had passed away a few years back. He had invited all his relatives for it. He assured me that he would it back early next day. He left in the evening as usual. We came to know of his death early morning the next day. A truck had broken down in the middle of the road. It did not have any reflectors. It seems Gaurav did not see it in time. From the look of the motorbikes' remnants, he must have crashed into it at a high speed. It was completely mangled and the whole road was full of his blood. I did not see his body personally but can you imagine what it must have looked like."

No, I wasn't thinking about the state the body was in. I was shocked. I was saddened by the fact that he was such a young lad, full of life with so much to look forward to.

"Did you know that when I had met Mr S.P.S. Oberoi last, he told me that Sarbat Da Bhala had started a campaign against sticker-less vehicles on highways of Punjab. In association with the Punjab Police, Sarbat Da Bhala got 25 lakh radium florescent stickers of various sizes to be stuck behind tractor trailers, buses and two wheelers. If only that truck had one of those stickers, Gaurav might have been saved." I said.

"He was always joking around with everyone. When he came for work, he wished everyone, including the old sweeper woman. Everyone excepting the old woman, reciprocated. Why she did not answer him was a complete mystery. After his death, the sweeper woman told me that he had accosted her about the fact that everyone reciprocated when he wished them, excepting her. He had said that he would be very happy if she responded when he wished her a good morning. She had assured him that in future, she would."

Ajit Pal gave a short sarcastic laugh. "That morning will never come now, not for her or Gaurav!"

Maybe, the sweeper woman knew his fate and did not want to become attached to Gaurav?

CHAPTER 15

It was a cold winter morning. The sun was hidden behind a thick blanket of fog. It was a beautiful sight. One could be sitting in Shimla or Kasauli. According to Teji, a hot cup of coffee is the least that that we could have to pamper ourselves on a day like this. I agreed because no patient was likely to come so early in the morning. In any case, we call these months part of the year 'healthy season'. The number of people reporting sick dwindles down to a mere trickle while emergencies due to heart attacks definitely rise.

As we ordered coffee, a bodybuilder type walked in. His upper arms had tattoos all over. He was wearing only a T-Shirt. His arms would easily be 17 inches in girth which was quite eye catching for a person who had been doing some weight lifting himself. His facial features told us that he does not belong to Punjab. He had with him a beautiful lady who also seemed to be a weight trainer. They sat on the other table and started eating the stuffed burgers that they had bought from the bakery. I was curious. I couldn't help looking at the lady knowing fully well that the weight lifter could easily cause great harm to me if he noticed my glances. Luckily, he had his back to me. I noticed how overweight people can also look nice if they are dressed properly. She was wearing a very snug fitting pair of jeans and a T-Shirt. The dress also greatly aggravated her assets. Comparatively, the two of us felt grossly overdressed. Looking at them, I conclude my thesis with the following remark:

When a person gets big and well developed muscles, he stops feeling cold.

When mortals like us are shivering in tweed coats and cardigans to boot, these people were so comfortable in T-Shirts. I was still wondering who the couple was.

As I take the first sip of the wonderful coffee, Teji informed me that some froth had decided to park itself in my moustache. I quickly cleaned the forth with a paper napkin. This has always been a problem with me and other Sikhs who have large moustaches. We can never eat ice cream in a cone! Neither can we have frothy coffee. I even eat mangoes with a spoon! Can you imagine? Mangoes are supposed to be sucked.

Anyway, as I cleaned my lips with a paper napkin, Teji said, "Just look at God's creation! The paper for the napkin that you just used, was the same that you used in the morning as toilet paper. Both are used to clean apertures in your body. God made sure that they are located at each end of your body!" and he laughed. The lady suddenly looked up and smiled. I don't know if the smile is meant for me or at what Teji had just expressed.

"Yes. You are right. Though one of the apertures uses recycled paper. The one I used is hopefully not recycled."

I saw four students sitting outside in a car eating Chinese food which they had ordered from the restaurant next to Monica's. After they finished eating, all four of them dumped the plates and the coke containers on the road from the car windows. They were laughing loudly and from the uniforms that they wore, I surmised that they belong to one of the best schools of Chandigarh. I watch them for some time. I couldn't control myself. I went up to them and said, "Are you kiddos from Vivek?"

One of them said, "Yes, Sir!"

"Is this trash yours?"

They looked at the trash they had created. From their expressions it seemed to me that they were definitely ashamed by their behavior. I asked them to pick everything up and throw it in the trash-bin provided. I came back inside. All four were again chatting and laughing and the trash was still where it was. After some time, they drove off leaving the scene.

"So what did you achieve?" Teji asked me.

"Nothing! I thought that they had some shame. I discovered that they don't. My job was to make them aware. Their ego forced them not to pick up the trash. Maybe, next time, they won't do it."

Just for the record, I discovered that everyone still throws their paper plates on the road in front of the many eating joints in that area, despite the fact that the establishments had put out trash bins. The ones who did this are the owners of large swanky cars and S.U.V.s who come out there to eat at all hours of the day. It has been three years since that incident. It just shows that people do not learn. Generations will change but these habits will not. The silver lining was that they were more people than before who threw their paper plates into trash-bins. I noticed that everyone who ate in places where they not served on their tables, picked up their plates or trays and put them where they were supposed to be kept. But when they were served on their tables, then they would automatically let their plates be.

That day, it seemed to me that Teji, who was normally a jolly person, was sad. I asked him why and he informed me that his uncle had died. He was his mother's sister's husband. We call him 'Masadji' in Punjab. As far as the hierarchy in family relatives goes, masar ji is way down, having hardly any say in matters of the in-law family. And this gentleman was 82 years old when he died. Naturally I was a bit surprised when I saw tears in Teji's eyes. He normally seemed to be a bit short on emotionalism. But then, there are all kinds of surprises in store for us. Maybe he had some special emotional attachment with the deceased. I asked him about his Uncle.

"You know, my brother Adarsh. He suffered from Juvenile arthritis and was an invalid since he turned three. My mother stayed with him in a hospital room for 18 years. I was junior to him by some years and was asked to stay with my mother's sister. That is how I came in touch with this man who has died today. He was my masi's (maternal aunt) husband. He was a simple man and he took me under his wing and treated me like a son. That is why I became attached to him."

My mouth was open and my jaws had dropped down to the floor.

"Adarsh stayed in a hospital room for 18 years? And your mother taught him to read and write, taught him languages and other stuff?" I asked.

"Yes. And he was curled up in the fetal position. She was the teacher, physiotherapist and mother, all rolled in one. Those days, I was an angry person for I thought that my mother gave all her love and affection to Adarsh and I was left out. Even when he started walking on crutches, I still nursed that grudge. As a fully grown man, he was just about four feet tall. He turned out to be one of the most adventurous persons I have ever known. You know, he brought in the first automatic Volvo car in Chandigarh. He drove it all the way from Europe in his physical state. I would have been scared just to venture out of the house! He was always very interested in music and photography. So he opened his studio in sector 17 and named it Adarsh Studio."

You know that at 4 feet nothing and in that physical state, he was married to lovely women. One was Afro-American lady who came all the way to India to get married to him. She even bore him a son who now lives in the U.S.A. They got divorced and then after some time, he married another lady who was 5 feet 8 inches tall. She bore him a lovely daughter. How he managed all that is itself a mystery."

My mind went to my association with Adarsh and the records that I bought from his studio. My last meeting with him was when I was called to see him. When I asked him what the problem was, he said, "Nothing Doc! I just feel very depressed."

I asked him if that was all that was bothering him. He replied in the affirmative. We talked about other things. He seemed better. He did not complain of any physical symptoms. After a short while I left. Half an hour later I was called back. He had asphyxiated in his own vomit, since he could not change sides on his own. That was the day when all the stiffness which had bothered him so much all through his life, deserted him in an instant. When I moved his arms, they were as supple and relaxed as any.

A few days ago, Teji put up a photograph of Adarsh on his wall on Facebook. I looked at it and a comment came immediately to my mind and I wrote, "MY FRIEND". I thought that about summed up all my feelings for him. He did not have to be a saint or a soldier to be my friend.

It was as if an era had come to an end.

CHAPTER 16

It was Diwali time. Diwali, the festival of lights, represented the victory of good over evil, when God Ram came home after trouncing Ravna, bringing a lot of hope to most people in India. Year after year, the traditions of Diwali are re-enacted in every Indian household. Teji's house was being painted as per those Diwali traditions. He had just come back from his studio in Sector 17, to check on shortages of painting material. More importantly, to see if the painters were on the job or not! The traditions of the past seem to have been pruned to a large degree in these inflationary times. If one does follow the modernized traditions, one must technically be loaded. Mulla (cash) should be pouring out of the ears. The exchange of sweets has given way to gifting of glassware, costly gifts, whiskey, wine and dry fruits. The prices of dry fruits have escalated at least four times in the last decade.

In my own case, I don't get the house painted during Diwali for two reasons. The artisans are mostly Muslim. They go back home or go on Haj during this period. So even if they are available, it is going to be a rushed affair. It also seems so copycat-ish. Nothing happens to the paint in a year, so why get under so much financial strain. The Goddess Laxmi will visit any abode if she has to. The traditional earthen lamps have given way to the Chinese electric laddees (strings of electric bulbs) as they are called.

For years, it was felt that the Goddess Laxmi finds her way to those households which are adequately lighted with the earthen lamps and candles. Her visits and her graciousness depend upon how well the houses are illuminated. Thus her visits to the poor were few and far between and they remained poor no matter how many Diwalis came and went. I have never witnessed a poor man become rich after Diwali. At least I did not become well off because of the Diwali lights and visits by the Goddess. Or did I? I *have* been lighting up my house fairly well. Maybe, the Goddess Laxmi liked my neighbors' illuminated house more, for he became infinitely richer than me. Nevertheless, the tradition goes on. The poor carry on spending whatever little they have saved on the fragile hope of a bonanza coming their way finally. The rich spend humungous amounts on gifts they have to shower on government officials whom they are duty bound to please. Diwali is just an excuse. The bigger the job, the bigger is the gift.

Goddess Laxmi, in the meantime, has become tech savy and will definitely visit those homes which have been illuminated by the jazzy electric lights from China instead of the Indian earthen lamps. Attitudes change with time.

Since I am not a government servant, I receive sweets only from my friends, though their number keeps dwindling with every passing year. I have been looking forward to some kind of bribe all my life, just to boost my ego, but none has come my way. Only I can tell you how small it makes me feel. I am not considered worth a bribe by any one!

My point of discussion is not Diwali. That day Teji came late for coffee because paint supply had to be replenished. Strange as it may seem, even I have no intention of having coffee at that point of time. But as I parked my car outside the clinic and was about to switch off the ignition, something told me to go and have coffee before I got down to serious business. Despite the fact that Teji had already had his daily cuppa, he still agreed to join me at Gelato. As we settled in, I was surprised to see my old friend Mrs. Bhatia outside the coffee shop. I waved out to her to come inside. I pulled up a chair for her.

Our conversation veers towards the new book, the one that you are presently reading. "What are you writing these days?" she wants to know. I summarize the book for her.

I ask her, "What should the next subject be, since I have finished writing about the Mr S.P.S. Oberoi?"

Her suggestion was spontaneous, "Write about Eunuchs! You have written enough about the rich and mighty. Come down to brass tracks. Write about these simple down trodden people who inhabit earth, the small and thickly populated chawls where they reside, the squalor and the dirt where they carry on their fight for survival. Write about these survivors. I can challenge the well-to-do to survive with them for a week. Write about the make shift jhuggis that they live in, the narrow lanes that automatically form as new chawls and jhuggis come up. Write about the eunuchs, the ones who have been the real sufferers of society for thousands of years. They have been ostracized by societies of all countries."

"You want me to write about eunuchs?" I asked, somewhat surprised. Who would want to read about them? They are ostracized indeed. The way they behave, any one would be more than willing to shun them.

"Yes! Why not? They are what they are for no fault of theirs. It is natures' fault. If someone has three fingers instead of five or if they have six fingers instead of five, would you treat them differently? There are people who have webbed feet. There are people with cardiac defects, cerebral defects, mongoloids. There are people with crinkly hair, black skins and flat noses. You don't treat them differently. So why are we treating these people with so much contempt and fear? Let me tell you that they are not as bad as you think they are. I know them pretty well!"

"Why should you be knowing anything about them?" I asked.

"It is because I am their legal counsel!" It was again my turn to open my eyes and mouth together in awe and surprise.

"Some years ago, I got to meet their chief whom they called Mummy ji. She resided in Mumbai. Remember, she was the head of the entire community of Eunuchs of the country. I asked my relatives in Mumbai about the place she lived in and the way to reach her. There was a lot of apprehension and they asked me to change my mind about going there. But I was very adamant. Finally I reached that area and asked a person to take me to her. He threw a barrage of questions at me, mainly about my motive. Once when he was satisfied that I was not some kind of a spy, he finally escorted me through narrow lanes of the chawl colony. I had never been to a place of that kind before. I was scared too. I had heard the same stories that you all have heard. We reached Mummy's chawl and was invited inside. She already knew that I was coming to see her.

After the initial pleasantries, we got to serious business to discuss various important things that I had come all the way from Chandigarh to discuss with her. She then announced that henceforth I was her chosen daughter. She presented me a sari and 1100 rupees as shagun (gift). She gave a suit for my husband and 1100 rupees and 1100 rupees for my son! After we had concluded our legal business, she asked one of her people to take me to a taxi and made sure that the driver rang her once I reached home safely. I kept in touch with her for many years but then she got murdered."

"Murdered? I thought you said she was the supreme head of the eunuch clan."

"Everyone has enemies. Maybe someone else wanted to take her place!" she said sadly.

"Are you in touch with them still?" I ask, strangely very intrigued by them.

"Yes, very much so, because, like I told you, I am still their legal council."

"What legal problems would eunuchs have? I mean why should they have any legal hassles?"

"And why not? They are normal people. They just have a physical abnormality like any other physically disabled person. They are very trust worthy, they have the same emotions as we do, they get angry as we do, maybe the swing would be a trifle too obvious, but they are very normal people. They are already fighting the world of the so called 'normal' people like us, where they have no identity of their own. That makes them very 'clannish' if you would care to call it that. They have properties, houses, their own fiefdoms, their families, their lovers and then their professional areas of dominance or you call them operational territories. They have disputes between themselves and with people of the 'normal' world. That is why they need someone like me, who is trying very hard to understand them, befriend them and then fight for them."

I came to know later that Mrs. Bhatia's family was like a family to them. The eunuchs went regularly to their house on festivals, sang and danced for them, blessed them and then in turn, Mrs. Bhatia generously gave them a lot of money.

I told them that the recent Pakistani movie 'BOL' had impressed me hugely. I had always held the view that the Pakistanis have no idea about movie making. One just can't sit through them even for ten minutes. But somehow, the title pulled me along. I went with my wife to the theater. There were only a few people in the hall and that too in the expensive seats. When

I saw it, my impression about Pakistani movies took a 180 degree spin. I asked Mrs. Bhatia if she had seen the movie. She had and her impression of the movie was the same as mine. She added that the movie was basically for the intelligentsia. I am happy that I was now included into that category. I slyly looked at Teji. He hadn't seen it. It was so obvious that I was intellectually superior at least to him. He had proven that notion wrong, time and again. But no longer.

Those of you who haven't seen it, let me take you through a tour of the movie. It is about a traditional healer (Vaid) living in Lahore. The entire cast and the director are Pakistani. It is a reverie of the eldest daughter who has been sentenced to death by hanging for killing her father, the Vaid, while she is on the scaffold. The hangman is put on hold by a decree from the President of Pakistan in response to a petition by her. She wants to tell her story to the press before she dies.

The story started with the Vaid facing turbulent times and a harsh future because of the changing scenario since medicine is progressing rapidly. Modern allopathic doctors had taken over the art of healing. The general public flocked over to them despite aggravated expenses. The Vaid's fertility quotient and his pining for a son goads him to produce more children till he has already sired six daughters. The wife was pregnant for a seventh time. Allah was happy with him this time, but only partially, for his wife gave birth to a son but with certain parts of his anatomy missing. So he is categorized a eunuch. The Vaid wanted to kill the child, but the wife denied him the right to do that. She insisted that she will bring the child up indoors and will not expose it to the outside world.

The child was pampered silly and brought up with great love by the sisters and he grows up to become a good artist. The father in turn abhorred him. A family friend insisted that he should be let out into the open so that he can paint. He takes him to a person who is into dolling up trucks in the true Pakistani tradition. That was where the sixteen year old came in. He got a job to paint the trucks in brilliant designs and colors.

The site where this young fellow was dropped off for work had a collection of weird men, who instantly latch on to the bonanza that has been offered to them on a platter. They begin drooling at the sight of him and one of the truck owners repeatedly observed "how tight this one is" at the sight of the lad. An opportunity came along when the owner of the shop went on an errand. Without wasting time, they gang raped the poor fellow with the engine revving at full throttle, and left him trussed up in the fields. Another eunuch who lived in that area rescues him and drops him off at his house.

The poor fellow narrates his woes to his mother when she asked him, "Why didn't you scream?"

He replied between sobs, "They had gagged me, mother!"

Unknown to the mother, the Vaid, was listening to his son. He understood the whole story immediately. He knew what the future held for his son. That night, he straddles his son as he slept and tried to suffocate him with a polythene bag over his head. The struggle put up by the boy wakes up the household but since the process was in motion, the Vaid decides to carry on despite the fact that the whole family was watching him. Their shrieking has no effect on him and soon the boy is still, motionless and quite dead. The Vaid had finally murdered his own son for whom he has had nothing but hate.

From then on, the animosity between father and daughter progresses by leaps and bounds. By a curious twist of fate, the Vaid is contracted to sire daughters from a beautiful dancing girl, a task he accomplishes easily. But then he does not want his daughter to grow up in the profession and tries to kill the baby. His daughter attacks her father with a stick to prevent him from murdering the baby girl. The Vaid dies as a result of his head injury and the daughter is convicted and sentenced to death. As she tells her story to the press, she is rapidly running out of time but manages to squeeze in her story despite the jailor wanting to finish off his job on time. As she finishes her story she shouts her message across in a simple sentence for the people of her country:

"Is a person who kills, a bigger criminal than a person, who goes on bringing unwanted children into this world?

She is hanged immediately after, for the President of Pakistan has denied clemency to her. This movie has shown the plight of such humans so poignantly and so effectively.

Down the ages, now that I think about it, eunuchs or pseudo hermaphrodites as they are often allured to as, have been put into positions of great trust by Queens and Monarchs alike. But they have always been maltreated too by most cultures. They have been reduced to objects of mirth and mockery and have been used in the entertainment industry. As a result they have relegated themselves to the background of society and are not seen as frequently as their numbers would deem them visible. The one country where they are overly visible is Thailand, where they have been incorporated into society by royal decree. They are offered all kinds of jobs and the entertainment industry is totally dependent on them. All of them have chosen to become women and have invested heavily in gaining womanly assets and as a result, some of them would give beauties of Thailand a run for their money.

"In France, Molin Rouge, the famous dance group totally consists of Pseudo-hermaphrodites. I am sure many men would opt for them instead." Teji let out a small chuckle.

I chip in with my inputs, "In Thailand, as you would know, the main industry is tourism. They also produce auto parts, computer hard ware, packed foods, etc. But the tourism industry remains the all time favorite. Prostitution is a word unheard of in that country despite the fact the 70 percent of the young women would, at a given time, be a part of the trade. What these young women do is not considered vile or inferior. They just work. Sex for money is work for them and is not frowned upon by society. They have mastered the art of pleasing males. To me it seems that it has permeated their very souls. They have different time schedules for the day. Since they work till late and then sleep late, they are out of circulation for the better part of the day. Then there are the amateurs who would never let a bargain go over their heads. They work for the most part in shops, parlors, their own shops and then double up as maids in bars. Nevertheless, the people of the third kind have a lot to offer the tourism industry."

"In India, they have a very different role. Indians generally are scared of them. There are stories about eunuchs castrating normal young men and pushing them into the homosexual prostitution trade. How far that is true is anyone's guess. Then we know that they have a spy system and they know about weddings, childbirths and in case a eunuch is born in their area. They are known to carry away the new born eunuch saying that it belongs to their community.

They should have come to our house on the birth of my grandson but for once, they missed out. In India, especially Punjab, the first Lohri festival for the male child is very auspicious. Thus we had a big party for which we had to pitch in a few tents and enclosures. That is what gave us away. News reached them and presto, the eunuchs of our area arrived and asked us when we would like to have them over.

"Come tomorrow" said my wife. There was no sense in denying.

They arrived in full strength the next day, at 4 p.m. as arranged. We welcomed them and served tea. We were informed that their "guru", Rita ji had been informed and she was on her way. We were given a visiting card which bore the picture of the Guru. It was on the next day that my wife read the card carefully and got a shock. It was clearly mentioned that if the ceremonies were held in the absence of the Guru ji, the ceremony would be held null and void and the gifting (badhai) would have to be done again! The ceremony started with two men on the harmonium and dholak (drum) respectively and the other three 'ladies' dancing and singing in tandem.

The negotiations were already in progress, even as they danced and sang. They wanted 1 lakh rupees and a diamond ring! They then came down to 51,000 and finally settled at 31,000 rupees. It did hit us, but then Rita ji explained the significance of it all.

She said, "Don't you realize the importance of the whole thing. You were lucky that you got married. You were luckier that you got a son and finally, you got a normal grandson who made you a Dada and Dadi (Paternal Grandparents). How many people are as lucky as you are? There are people who don't get married, don't have children, don't have sons and then don't have grand children. Look at us. We will never get married or have children, but we go to dance and sing at weddings and child births, showering blessing on everyone. Things are getting expensive and we have to survive, no?"

Once the basics had been sorted out, they showered rice and blessing into the house and upon the occupants of the house, sang, hugged everyone, posed for photographs and left happily.

When they had gone, we sat and pondered over the issue and then accepted the whole thing as a part of life.

Vikramjit wrote on my wall, "I am waiting. When will the eunuchs come to my abode? I am dying for the day I become a DADA!"

CHAPTER 17

There are people who have perpetually spinning wheels under their feet. Thus travelling is an obsession with them. I agree that this hobby costs money, but there are many people with money who don't travel at all. In India, residents of the states of Gujarat and Bengal are compulsive travelers.

Teji is also like that. His wife is equally fond of travelling and globetrotting which was a huge advantage for him. He was off on one of his routine jaunts around the world. Six months back, he had gone on a 14 day bus journey across Turkey with his wife. They covered about 4,500 kms in that time. The year before that, he had gone on an Alaskan ferry trip. This time around, he had gone on a bus trip to Sweden, Holland and probably Austria. So that leaves me alone for coffee.

I invited Jagtar to have coffee with me. I noticed that someone had kept his laptop on my table. I sat on the other table but soon realized that the person to whom the laptop belonged was none other than my friend and fellow golfer, Vikramjit Singh. After making a killing in counter trading in Mumbai, he had settled in Chandigarh. He was leading a semi-retired life. Being a very likable fellow, he jelled with golfers of all age groups. Since he was in the Golf Club a lot, youngsters called him a 'permanent fixture', just like Teji and I were 'permanent fixtures 'in the Gelato.

"I was just wondering who had left his laptop and gone away!" I said, somewhat relieved.

"I tend to finish my work here while I am on a coffee. I had to go the toilet, so I just told this guy to look after my laptop while I was away." he explained.

We indulged in discussions on various subjects and small talk when in walked Jagtar. After the usual pleasantries, we got to talking about the corruption in the country and the people who had made it large in the country and how. We know who all those people were. As we were performing live autopsies on all and sundry, the living and the dead, Sam's Kanwal, wife walked in and kindly consented to have a cold coffee with vanilla ice cream. As she settled down, a politician's son passed by in the corridor. He had been accused of raping his 53 year old maid. I wondered aloud if he really did it. Raping a 53 year woman by a man who could lose everything that the family had worked for seems rather farfetched. Anyway, the court had acquitted him.

But society had already passed its' own judgment and such judgments usually are there to stay, irrespective of what the courts had decreed. In this case, society had pronounced him guilty even before the trial. Hence sitting in the coffee parlor, we had introduced him to Sam's wife, not by his name but by what he was supposed to have done!

Society is very unforgiving. It also has a very long memory.

She soon finished her coffee and after thanking us profusely, she excused herself. Jagtar also had to go. That left the two of us alone

"This friend of mine who you just met is Jagtar Singh? Do you have any idea about how great a man he is? He is a man in hurry. And do you know why? He has to reach home at six in the evening. Because he has a wife at home who is a vegetable. She does not react, she does not converse, she passes her stools and urine in her clothes. If one feeds her, she eats. She will die if Jagtar is not there. She falls frequently and hurts herself. She gets epileptic fits. Jagtar rushes home to look after her at six. He cleans her, changes her clothes, washes them and then puts them out to dry. When he has tucked her in, he opens his booze bottle and by 9 o'clock, when his wife has had dinner and is sleeping, he is drunk himself. Only then can he sleep. He sleeps till 12 a.m. in the night when it is time for him to change his wife's clothes, feed her, give her medicines, and put her off to sleep again. The time is 4 a.m. by then. That is the time he can go off to sleep himself. He has been doing this every day for the last 10 years of his life. He is 62 years old. His wife is 60. Her name is Veena. You have seen the fellow Arjun, the beggar boy who keeps going up and down on his legs all curled up under him, deformed beyond repair?" I asked.

"Yes!"

"Kalil Gibran, the Syrian philosopher had said *"Your children are not your children. They are through you but not of you. All you have to do is to guide them like arrows towards their destiny"* I wonder why God keeps testing families who have deformed children and family members, whom they have to look after for the rest of their lives.

With that, we decided to call it a day. But my mind was in a turmoil once again. I thought about Jagtar Singh and wondered at the kind of life that he was living. He had no life of his own. I still remember the time he fought a dozen hoodlums single handedly, armed only with a weapon which was between a sickle and a short sword. He had to go in and save his employers' son-in-law and his family because he was supposed to have molested the wife of a local Don, who had decided to kill all of them. His employer had sent in a posse of policemen but they did not want a situation. The don had armed men on roof tops of neighboring buildings. Not caring for his personal safety and ignoring the pleas from the police posse, he went in and got the entire family out. How he did all that is another story. His employer offered him a bottle of booze for his efforts which Jagtar declined.

Another time, he got into an altercation with a group of milk vendors who would come honking their rubber horns at five in the morning when everyone was asleep outdoors. An infuriated Jagtar Singh with his hair flowing all over, decided to take them on. He overturned their milk drums. The fight that ensued was something out of a Bollywood movie. But then that was Jagtar Singh. And now, when his wife got an epileptic fit, he howled in uncontrolled panic, with tears flooding the room! He can't think of a life without her, despite the fact that she does not talk to him and is hardly an ideal companion in anyone's dotage.

"At least she can hear me. So what if she can't talk to me. She understands what I say to her. I understand her garbled speech. She is there. That is all that matters to me." he said.

I am sure it was not a fairy tale love story all the way. They must have had their share of marital tiffs. What would I have done had I been in Jagtar's shoes? Isn't it easy to give unsolicited advice? Who knows?

For the time being, I thank God for what I have been given by him and I thank God for what he will give me in future!

CHAPTER 18

I came to know Drish Sandhawalia as a golfer from the Chandigarh Golf Club, then as a patient in the clinic and finally as a friend and a coffee mate in the Gelato Ice cream parlor. In all scenarios, I found him to be a complete gentleman, though his wife might differ on that count, for wives have different views about their husbands. After all, they get a million more opportunities to get to know the man better. When two ordinary people meet, each one puts his best foot forward to impress the other person. After a prolonged interaction, they get to see each other's faults. If the two get over that period, they get to become friends. But in a marriage scenario, the two get to see the well behaved aspect of the relationship during the engagement phase and then the bomb explodes once they begin living together. They see the woman without her mascara and makeup, her inability to cook or be a good hostess, the smelly mouthed man, the unruly hair, and wonder if this was really the person they had agreed to get married to? Irrespective of subsequent views they might hold about each other, they have to stay together as friends, at least in the Indian setup.

Drish is a soft spoken and an extremely well read computer expert. We would meet over a cup of coffee and soon became good friends. Then his family started coming to me as patients and that is how I met his father, Mr Preminder Singh Sandhawalia. If I call Drish a gentleman, then his father qualified to be called a super gentleman.

Our friendship blossomed over the years and so did the family's trust in me as their family doctor. Mr Sandhawalia would ring me from England if he had a minor problem. A thing like Atrial Fibrillation which even a medical student could diagnose became an object of fascination for him and he never would miss a chance to tell everyone that I was the first person to diagnose his Atrial Fibrillation! Mr Sandhawalia was bestowed a peer ship in London which made him the Lord of Redwick.

Drish has a younger brother, Birinder, alias Bunny, who lives in London and is a research fellow in multi specialties. He had a PhD which gave him the title of 'Doctor'. I am telling you this because of an event which recently took place in London. He purchased a flat in London and invited his parents to come and stay with him for a few days. Mr Sandhawalia, his dad, was a frequent visitor to London but this time the cold and clammy weather got to him. After being diagnosed as a case of chest infection, he was put on treatment but four days later, he died of a cardiac arrest. The ambulance arrived within three minutes of the emergency call. The paramedics did all they could do, but to no avail. Mr Sandhawalia had gone out on his feet. He was there one moment and gone the next. The precipitating factor was Pneumonia.

Drish flew out to London and the two brothers brought Mr. Preminder Singh Sandhawalia home. The customary rituals took place according to Sikh rites. A beautiful and touching eulogy was read by his brother-in-law. Two days later, Birinder came to my clinic seeking my help for a funny feeling he had in his chest. On examination, I discovered that he was absolutely fine. I reassured him and soon the inevitable happened. The topic of his father's death came up. Birinder, who is a good golfer himself, opened up to me with his innermost feelings.

He said, "Doc! You know, I had been wanting to tell my dad how much I loved him, how much I admired him as a human being and for being such a wonderful father; a father who had never raised his voice in anger. He had never criticized anyone in his life, neither had he ever a bad word for anyone. But I could not say anything of the kind to him. I thought my Dad would start wondering what had gone wrong with me, because I had said nothing for 40 years, so why now? I had never even hugged him, despite the fact that I was aching to do so. For that matter, the only physical contact that he had with me was an occasional brush of his hand on my shoulder or a pat as he passed my chair."

I agreed with him and said, "I know, I know. It is said that *'the saddest tears are shed over the things that we never said and the hug that we never gave'*. But in the Indian set up, how many of us hug our children or any of our loved ones. It is understood and taken for granted that we love them and that we are loved, so the physical confirmation is never required. Or so we think. I have often wanted to hug my son, but things get so awkward that he ends up touching my feet and I end up shaking hands with him in a man to man gesture. The father and son hug has never come. I remember only one occasion when my mother put her arm around me as I sat on the bed. I was thirteen years old then. I was on a strike because of a comment that my father had made. On the other hand, in western cultures, the hug comes so easily, as if that is the most natural thing to do to one another. It is a different matter if the hug actually means anything to either party. The phrase, 'I love you', used by them so often, one wonders if it is a just a figure of speech and in most cases, it stays that way, a figure of speech!" Indians never say it.

Birinder was hurting for the things that he wanted to say to his father but could not and did not. For a son, these were things which opened old wounds again and again. It would take some time to heal, if at all.

"You know Doc? In the UK, they keep the bodies in a place they call a 'Chapel'. In India we have the morgues where we they pile bodies one on top of another in a refrigerated container. In some places they have regular compartmentalized pull-out stretchers. But in this Chapel, the atmosphere was so serene. Someone had put on hymns from Sikh scriptures which played softly in the background. They normally dress up the deceased in his or her best clothes, even paint them up with rouge, the full works. We don't respect our dead as they do. We can't wait to put them on the ground."

We put the deceased down on the floor the moment he dies, as if no one can bear to see the dead on a bed. He has to return to the dust from where he arose as quickly as possible.

"Doc, why do we do put the dead body on the ground the moment a person dies? Anyway, the Director of the chapel called me aside. When we were alone, he whispered to me, as if he did not want to wake up the dead!" He laughed sardonically and carried on "No, no. I was joking. He probably whispered out of respect for the deceased, not wanting to spoil the solemn atmosphere of the place by talking loudly! He asked me how I was related to the deceased. I told him he was my father."

"Ah!" he said and carried on, "You know, Sir! I have been doing this for over thirty years. So I know what I am talking about. When dead people come here, their bodies are all taut. Their hands and feet are stretched and twisted. Some have painful grimaces on their faces. But in my thirty years plus experience I have never seen a more peaceful person in death, as your father. His hands and feet were as supple as if he was sleeping. I surmised that he was a very noble soul. I just thought that I should share this with you."

"Doc! He then shook hands with me and once again condoled with me and before moving again, he added, 'I have never said these words to anyone before.' And he left. I could only say, "Yes, he was a noble soul!" Doc, this day had to come sometime. But there is a thought at the back of my mind that he could have stayed with us for some more years. We could have learnt so much more from him."

"It is all pre-ordained. No one can do anything about it. And let me tell you something. Today, you were suffering from nothing serious which warranted my attention. I think your soul had to let out your feelings and pain. It was just that you had to tell me something about your father and the feelings of a son. You had to come to me so that I can write about him. Be sure that I will. *It will probably be a lesson for other sons and fathers to tell each other that you love them and not let it all be left as an "understood fact of life"!*

My mind went back to my own father. I was thinking of the hug. We were a 'together' kind of a family. We went to the Services Club, swam, played badminton and table tennis together. We travelled all over town on bicycles. We went rafting down the Narbada river which passed through the marble rocks of Jabalpur. But he was also strict as a strict father should be. We were on the receiving end of a leather belt on one or two occasions. It hurt but then I suppose that was required in those times. It is not that we were scared of him because the belt came out only once in a while. My mother was equally strict when the occasion demanded. The hugs never came and neither were they expected. They did not matter, for we loved our parents unconditionally and so did they. The love that the parents nourished us with was so obvious that we probably did not need those reassuring hugs. That was the general trend in the Indian family set up.

But that was not true for my mother and her mother, my grandmother. I remember when we went to Srinagar for our annual holidays, where my grandparents resided, the scene on the bus stand would turn absolutely chaotic because the two would hug each other and wail loudly without a care in the world, for what seemed to us as an eternity. For them, all that mattered was the hug and the crying which drowned all their sorrows or happiness on meeting each other again. Was it a Kashmiri ritual? They conveyed their deep love for each other through those acts. People looked on in awe and wondered who had died. We as children would look at each other and at them and wonder if it was something that we did that had brought on that reaction. The hugging stopped the moment they reached home and they resumed their usual arguments. There were no recurrences of hugging while we were on our vacations. It was only when we were supposed to leave for home that the same performance was repeated at the bus stand and it was abandoned only when the driver threatened to leave without us. This ritual remained consistent for years till my grandmother died.

That hugging ritual was not repeated for us. It baffles me. Was it because we were boys and boys did not deserve that kind of hugging? My mother never hugged my grandfather in the same way as she hugged my grandmother. The bonding between the two ladies was so deep that when my mother was involved in an accident where her elbow was shattered into tiny bits which had to be screwed together. The good doctor, Dr. Pardaman Singh did a wonderful job, but she was in pain for a long time. I remember my Grandmother getting severe pains in exactly the same location for which she had to keep on tying bandages and taking pain relievers. And all this while she was in Bangalore and my mother was in Chandigarh! Distance did not seem to matter.

These days, mothers and fathers hug their children all the time and the children still don't have any deep emotional bonding. *In golf, we say that the drive is for show; the putt is for the dough.* Today, children don't reach the putting stage for they are only like the drive. They are for show. They are sent out to expensive boarding schools where they stay till the beginning of their college days and then go on to the careers they choose. Parents are shadows whom they encounter only now and then. The 'putting' never really happens. If something bad happens with the child, the parents are always available for the blame game. The children can always say that parents were not available when they were needed. Then there is the omnipresent society which can be blamed for creating such conditions where they could not get a good job or cough up good role models. And then there is the all time favorite, stress, which pushed them into alcoholism or drugs.

Does it seem to you that I am saying that hugging or telling the other party that you love them does not matter in today's scenario? It does. Indians should resort to this practice because we are basically an emotional lot. We care about our children and parents in a very positive sort of a way. Hugging just sends out signals which confirm what we actually feel. It can tell them how much they are loved, I am sure it will only add to those emotions. But in the Indian scenario, one can hug friends easily, without giving it a second thought but hugging parents and siblings seems such an embarrassing act. Mothers resort to hugging when the children are younger. It is felt that the father's authority is mitigated if he gets mushy with children. Hence he maintains his distance. I suppose that is why the act of touching the feet of parents and elders was started.

This act of touching the feet of elders gained more importance because showing 'respect' was thought to be greater than demonstrating 'love'. In a particular sect in India, everyone is supposed to touch each others' feet. It does sound strange but you see a 90 year old man touching the feet of a 5 year old. Maybe it is to say that all human beings are equal, irrespective of their ages? So hugging should demonstrate equality too, would it not?

I got a jolt when Mr Kiran Dutta, a young I.T. scientist from Andhra Pradesh, came in for his medical while I was writing this piece. He told me that in the south of India which was constituted by the four states of Andhra Pradesh, Karnataka, Kerala and Tamil Nadu, the concept of touching anybody's feet is non—existent! I couldn't believe it.

"So how do you greet your parents when you are leaving on a journey? I will touch my mothers' feet if I have to go on any journey and also on my return."

"No Sir!" he said, "I have never touched their feet. We just say namaskaram! That is all."

One of my relatives forbade my grandson from touching his feet because he felt that we are all divine. Hence no one should touch anyone's feet.

That was food for thought. I am still mulling over the subject.

CHAPTER 19

THE EULOGY

I was sitting alone at the coffee parlor that day and I was thinking about death, mine in particular. Death might seem to you a very morose, repulsive or even a perverse subject to talk about. But at the end of the day, one has to agree that it is something very real. It happens to real people. In my profession, you just can't run from it or even turn your face away when you see it approaching someone. Obviously, it hasn't approached me yet. But I have thought about it many times. I am sure most of you have too. Some people might even be obsessed about it in the sense that they want it to stay as far away from them as possible. They are too scared of dying. Just the thought of a world without them scares the hell out of them. This is despite the fact that out of all the scariest things that man has ever dabbled in, dying does not take the coveted top slot. It is public speaking that takes the numero uno position! Then there are people like me who are not scared of dying at all. Maybe, we lie. But we are definitely scared of *how* we will die! It is also said that people are not scared of dying per se', but of being *forgotten* after they die.

I wonder why people are scared of dying. They will go to heaven or they will go to hell. They don't realize that these are the only two places which welcome you with open arms. There must be a sign at the entrance which says "*Jee aayan nu*" which in English means that "You are most welcome!" No one is asked to go back saying that there was no previous booking or the director has to be asked before someone is allotted accommodation. There is no preferential treatment meted to a King, a President or a pauper.

On a personal level, I believe that heaven and hell are of our own making. They exist here on earth. You don't have to die to go to heaven or hell. Everyone pays his or her debts here, before they die. It is the way one has lived that decides if your living life is heaven or hell. But then where does the soul go once it escapes this body? It just can't wander around looking for likeminded souls or for ones who fall into a special category depending upon what they have done while they were on earth.

In my life, as I have already confessed, dying has always loomed large in the scheme of things. As a teenager, I was petrified by the imagery of leading my own funeral procession in the supine position, very dead of course. That was fine with me. The thing that bothered me immensely was the number of people who would be present in the funeral procession. Somehow, there weren't ever enough people. I was also scared that out of the few people who would come, no one would show any impressive degree of grief. Didn't they know that I was gone and that I would no longer be around anymore? I knew that there would be some relieved ones too. Some of them would even be happy for I had made some enemies too. It was then that I would foolishly break into a sweat.

The question that the voice inside me asked was "So how does it make a difference? You are already dead!

How does the number of people following you to the cremation ground matter? And how does it matter to you if anyone is relieved or happy when you cop it? Sahir Ludhianvi, the famous poet from Punjab, in his song 'Jadon meri arthi . . . .' says that in my funeral procession, my friends will be crying but some enemies would be humming a happy tune." Somehow, no matter how the inner voice explained the futility of the numbers in the funeral, it mattered to me in the nightmare and it still matters when I am awake.

What then is the use of having lived an unappreciated life?

Sometimes, I feel that enough is enough. I am 64 years old. I have done this, been there. But then a question always pops up, "How much is enough?" When one is bored of doing the same things again and again, meeting the same people in weddings, asking the same mundane questions "So how is life treating you?" or "What else is happening?" or the all time favorite, "Haven't seen you in ages?" it makes you wonder if going to these occasions is a necessity? Then you go to a funeral and even as they light the pyre, you see people laughing and discussing almost every topic that should not be discussed in that scenario. Don't you see that the family of the deceased is watching your behavior? But it doesn't affect anyone. Perhaps the family is relieved that at least people came for the funeral, even if they are discussing the value of gold which has touched Rs. 31,500 per gram or the sensex is hovering around 21,000, or even some new scam that has surfaced! After all, the trip to mars cost a whopping Rs. 4500 crore.

In our scenario, being seen at bhogs is very important. It doesn't matter if you knew the departed well enough. Society demands your presence. Your standing in society also depends upon the number of times you were spotted at funerals and if not at the funeral, at the bhog ceremony. Moreover, if you were seen a hundred times at such events, the chances are that there will be enough people at your own bhog ceremony, whenever that may be. The popularity that the deceased had enjoyed in society is also directly proportionate to the number of people present. This has been ordained by society. As I grew older and became a part of a society which took funerals and bhog ceremonies seriously, I too started attending them. I saw people who professed to be very close to the family or to the guy who had copped it, get up to speak at the end of the ceremony for the eulogy. Most of them were accomplished speakers as if they were politicians. The number of people saying a eulogy for the departed and the length of their eulogies also mattered gravely.

As a fall out, a recent thought that has been bothering me is my eulogy that will be said when I come under the category of "the departed soul". So who will say mine? Who will that person or persons be, who will speak about me at my bhog (the ceremony that is conducted at the Gurudwara for the peace of the departed soul) ceremony?

I am certain of one thing. There won't be a stampede of people wanting that job.

I will have to make a personal request to the few friends that I have before I die. At least that will ensure their presence. My problem is that I have many acquaintances, but very few friends. I am not the flower which beckons all the birds and bees, with my nectar. I am not even the honey which is the collective labor of love of a thousand bees. I am a paradox. The world around me thinks that I have a wide base of friends and that I am very popular. What they do not know is that I am actually a loner.

I do have a few quality friends. The best part of this situation is that I can count them upon my fingers.

This makes life so much easier. But which friend will I call upon to say my eulogy. I have to decide which of my friends knows me well enough or me him.

Which of these friends remembers me well enough to leak out my hidden cache of good deeds, say all the good things that my soul will long to hear on that day, impressing all the people who would grace my bhog ceremony, hordes or a handful?

All these things do matter. Because what will be said from my friend's heart will be the summary of my life. Selecting the one friend who will say my eulogy is definitely going to be a tough ask, for they are all deserving. When one is younger, one selects friends randomly. There are no special criteria or a list of qualities which we use as a tick off list to make friends. It is just the heart which does the job. It tells us who it likes and would like as a friend. Then it depends upon that person to reciprocate. At least in my case, I have never made a friend according to his social standing or how rich his parents were and then maybe how he could prove to be helpful to me, some day in my life. No wonder I have never been in the name throwing business. Anyway, the last criteria never came into play when we were young because what anyone will ultimately turn out to be was still a mystery.

It is odd, that I still remember my first two friends. I am not good at remembering names as Sam is, but I remember Ravi Sharma's name clearly. We must have been 9 or 10 years old, studying in St. Aloysius School in Kanpur. His father was the driver of our school bus. My mother knew about him and his background but looked after him well whenever he came to our house. I don't remember a single moment when she allured to his background or made him remotely conscious of the obvious difference in our social standing. She offered goodies that she used to make herself but she never told me to choose friends from a different class,(read 'upper class!')

I remember having gone to his house only once. He had been very insistent. It was a very hot and humid day. They lived on the school premises in quarters provided to them by the school. It was a small house. I remember his mother offering a glass of plain water with a table spoon of sugar stirred well. It was an ordeal to drink that concoction but then thanks to the way we were reared, I drank it all displaying much feigned pleasure. That had made Ravi's mother happy. It was later that I wondered why they did not have orange squash or even a lemon at home because a bar of Cadbury's chocolate cost only 25 paisa in those days. Hence a lemon would have been less than peanuts. It would have been easily affordable even on a driver's salary of those days. My memory is blurred about the reasons why we could not maintain our friendship. I had changed my school initially and then my father got posted out of Kanpur. If my mother had advised me to choose friends of higher standing, maybe I too could have thrown big names today as quite a few of my acquaintances do. But then such friendships come with a price tag upon them and one has to suck up to these 'friends' unless one is a Gandhi or an Ambani. It is something that is expected out of you because you are the sucker. In my case, thankfully, I was never required to be a sucker. We were all equal in each other's eyes, at least in those days.

My other friend was Vira Sibal. I met him after I left St Aloysius School and joined college. He was a plump, happy go lucky fellow and in contrast to Ravi, he was from a very rich family of Kanpur. I wasn't in his league but we clicked. We went to NCC camps together, took the night patrolling in the same shift. We visited each others' homes regularly. We were in contact till a few years ago. Their family sort of broke up when a property dispute arose between the two brothers. But we still have common friends and I am sure we will meet again.

It is not that I belonged to a rich family. We were a displaced family from Pakistan. When the dreaded partition of India took place in 1947, my father lost all his material assets in the great and terrible border crossing. Escaping with their lives, they relocated in

India. My mother's family, who were not known to my father yet, settled down in Srinagar and my father's family settled in Delhi. My father took up a job in the Army Ordinance Corps and was posted in Aptabad for starters. I was born later in 1949. Thank God for small mercies. Otherwise I would not have been sitting here writing about my friends and grappling with the issue of choosing the right friend for my eulogy. In those days of mass murder, there were no eulogies that were said for millions of people. Most of them did not even have funerals. There were only mass cremations for the ones left over by the buzzards and dogs.

I am luckier, for at least I have the hope and the choice of a friend who will eulogize me. The only unanswered question still is: Who will that person be?!

CHAPTER 20

"Oye Daactar-aaa! Where were you last evening? I wanted you to come over for a drink at my house! I have won that case which was in court for the last 21 years! We were celebrating. The court's judgment came out yesterday!"

Teji made an animated entry in Gelato. The Punjabis have a funny habit of prolonging a name or word just like Teji did with 'Doc'! If we have to call out to a guy named Rakesh, we would say, Rakayshe-aaa!. It sounds more affectionate.

"Congratulations! I was in the Gurudwara!" I replied.

"Whom are you trying to impress? Don't I know you? Sau choohey kha kar billi haj ko challi!" he said. (after devouring a hundred mice, the cat is off on a pilgrimage.)

"I have been doing that for some time now. You know I have never been the Gurudwara *type*. But recently, whenever I finished my clinic, and passed in front of the Gurudwara on my way home, a strange kind of guilt seemed to goad me to stop and go inside. A voice seems to say to me, "You can go to a friend's house, but when it comes to paying a visit to your best friend's house, you find a thousand things to do." I succeeded in bypassing it many times, but I finally succumbed to the inevitable. For years, I have been advising my alcohol dependant patients that they can easily kick the habit by going to the Gurudwara or their temple during the 7p.m. to 9 p.m. slot when the urge really gets to them. By the time one is over that period, the urge to drink is gone. No one listened to my advice. Neither did I, for I never thought myself to be alcohol dependant. I just looked forward to two drinks of my own. Now that I don't care too much for the drinks myself, it was easier for me to take up my own advice. Wonder of wonders, I started liking it. Soon I got into the groove of the time slot. People started recognizing me in the Gurudwara.

One gentleman came up to me and said, "It is good that your mind is now turning towards God!"

You know what the best feeling that came with it was? I became a member of the 'Saadh Sangat', people who came in to listen to the Guru's words. They were all good people. Just like golfers, who have only one aim in life, to put the ball into the hole. Here everyone had one aim in life or at that point of their lives: to be one with the Lord."

I saw Teji looking at me sideways, trying to analyze me. He was wondering if I had actually lost it.

I carried on in the same vein, "After I thought I was in a groove, another thought ate my head off. The voice, which was obviously my conscience reminded me that all Sikhs are supposed to donate ten percent of their earnings to the Gurudwara. So I started doing that on a daily basis, for giving 10 percent over a month or a year would have proved to be a big ask. I would have definitely changed my mind. So I settled into a daily

10% sort of 'donation'. It included what one puts into the coffers for 'matha tekna', the money for the 'parshad' and last but not the least, to the bards or the 'ragis' who sing the Lord's hymns, for it is they who acquaint the Saadh Sangat with the teachings of the Guru Granth Sahib!"

"I am impressed. What if you really have something else to do, like coming to my house for a drink?"

"Oh! In that case, I shall do whatever is needed in the Gurudwara as usual and then nip over to your place. But there are days when one just can't go. Then one asks for forgiveness and goes whenever one can. Do you remember the sector 8 Gurudwara in the 60's?"

"How can I? We live right across the Gurudwara. Moreover, my father and a few of his friends were in charge of the one room place."

"Yes! When we came to Chandigarh after my father's death in 1966, his elder brother, Major Hardit Singh used to live in Sector 8. I still remember him saying that to begin with, he was alone and then he got married and became two. They then went on to make 7 babies and became 9. Thus their house number can be memorized very simply-129! Because we were very close to them, we would come to celebrate all Gurpurabs in sector 8. There were a few people in those days. The langar was fantastic, as always." I reminisced.

"And slowly the Gurudwara was expanded and it has become what it is today."

"There was a tree in the courtyard and the langar was served around it. I wonder when it was chopped down. This Gurudwara is also known as Dasveen Padshayee Gurudwara. That means Guru Gobind Singh Sahib, the 10th Guru of the Sikhs, must have come here during one of his travails."

"You know, Doc! The deed papers to the Gurudwara were in the name of Sardar Diljang Singh Johar, my father. Before his death, he called me over and handed the papers to me and told me that I should hand the papers only to a person who is completely reliable. Otherwise, some unscrupulous person might even sell the Gurudwara! After he died, I made zerox copies of the documents and put them in the money box, with a note attached that the original documents would be handed over to a responsible committee. They contacted me and I handed the documents over to the committee. A person who lives next to the Gurudwara has filed a case against the Gurudwara!"

"Wonderful!" I said sarcastically, "Can this be done? Can a house of God be sold?"

"If one man can sell off his wife and children, then selling God and the house of God is easy. And this fellow happens to be a Sikh!"

As I sit in the serene atmosphere of the Gurudwara, following the translation of the hymns from Gurmukhi to English on the giant screens and in the computer screen behind which I usually sit, one learns to read the script too. My speed of reading the Gurmukhi script is pathetically slow. My father was in the army, as I have already told you. We shunted all over the country excepting the Punjab. Hence whatever Gurmukhi that I learnt was not in school but at home.

I notice that the same people come in every evening. Everyone, including me, had developed a fixed routine once they walk through the door of the hall. They walk down the center at varying speeds with different expressions on their faces, mostly of reverence and then come down to bow in front of the Holy Granth Sahib. One is supposed to touch ones' forehead to the ground. Everyone takes a round of the pedestal, on which is seated the Guru Granth Sahib, touching their fore heads in places which their habit dictates, before finally settling down cross-legged in their chosen places in front of the ragis. Some people leave after the initial sequence. A lot of them realize that they are supposed to go out retreating, facing the Guru Granth Sahib and not with their backs towards it because showing their backs means showing disrespect.

I noticed that there are a lot of young boys and girls who come to pay their respects. Quite a few of the boys have their hair chopped. It is such a shame. I suppose they have opted for the easy way out or they have examples in the family whom they follow. I personally dislike the trend because the 'form' or the 'roop' (form) of the Khalsa (the pure) is the primary requirement of Sikhs. If you can't maintain your 'roop' which consists of the unclipped beard, unshorn hair and the turban, then you just can't maintain the other requirements. And who said that it is easy to truly follow the tenets of any religion, may it be Sikh, Hindu, Jewish, Muslim or Christian. But the young ones are revolting against strict rules of religion. I also feel that in the olden days, since Sikhs invited the enemy to partake langar (food partaken in a group in the Gurudwara), then why should such people, who have not maintained their 'roop' be ostracized and criticized and ultimately shooed away from their parent religion. They can be coaxed back when realization dawns on them, and they will be the devout in the full form of the Khalsa.

Initially girls who came into the Gurudwara wearing jeans and revealing clothes were frowned upon. Not now, for I see most of the young girls who come in, wear jeans. They come in droves. If they have to go home to change into a more appropriate attire after being in jeans the whole day, then chances are that they might skip the idea of visiting the Gurudwara totally. These are the future of our religion for they are the ones who will teach their children about their religion and the need to visit the Gurudwara.

I am an exception for I sit behind the Guru Granth Sahib, behind the man handling the computer translations of the shabads (the hymns) as they were being sung by the ragis. I could not sit in the cross legged posture or the lotus posture for more than a minute, for my hip joints, thighs and knees would start aching. Moreover, I needed a wall to rest my back on. Now, with practice, I have reached 45 minutes to an hour in the lotus posture.

My mind wandered down memory lane and I wondered why, after I reached maturity, did I begin to cry the moment I went down the stairs of Harmandir Sahib (Golden Temple) in Amritsar to get my first glimpse of the sacred Gurudwara, the Akal Takhat? I still shamelessly do that. So do many more devotees! These are tears of happiness and gratitude. Gratitude, for making me what I am (a Sikh) and happiness at being made the chosen one who has the good fortune of visiting the most sacred of all institutions of the Sikhs. Incidentally, the Harmandir Sahib or the Golden Temple is the only Gurudwara in the world which has been built at a lower level than the ground. One goes down some twenty or thirty steps to reach the level of the Golden Temple.

And why did the Japanese doctor, who had no idea what Sikhism was or what the Harmandir Sahib stood for. He had just come to meet Ludhiana's Dr Iqbal Singh, the pioneer of the test tube baby in India. He began to shed tears uncontrollably in the inner sacred sanctorum, all the while standing on one leg because there was no place to put the other one down? Dr Iqbal Singh had no forthright answer to the good Japanese doctor's question "Dr Singh, why am I crying?" No one had forced him to go to the Akal Takhat or donate money all over. He had no knowledge about the Sikh religion as such. Since he was in Ludhiana, which is just one hour away from Amritsar, he had asked to see the Golden Temple for it is a monument known all over the world.

So why did his tears flow incessantly in the Golden Temple?

The construction of the Harmandir Sahib was completed in the year 1601. The Guru Grath Sahib was installed in the Harmandir Sahib by the 5th Sikh Guru, Guru Arjan Dev ji, who invited Baba Budha ji as the first granthi (head priest) of the Golden temple. These hymns have been sung in the Harmandir Sahib for more than 413 years, through day and night, till the Guru Granth Sahib is taken to the resting place for the night! What can be expected after such cleansing of the atmosphere and the souls of the devout? The vibes are undilutedly pure.

That is what produced the tears of happiness and reverence in the Japanese doctor despite being totally ignorant of the Sikh faith. I am sure that after that experience, his life must have been affected for the better.

In the meantime, the hymn being sung was," Since mankind was made by the Lord from the same light, how can someone be good and someone be bad?". There was another one, "Now, then, when, now, it is you, it is you, it is you, my Lord!"

I realize most of the hymns are in praise of the Lord and the Guru Granth Sahib. The next one is "Vaho, Vaho Guru Gobind Singh, Apey Guru, apey chela . . ."

My routine had included a stupid point. I used to get up as the last hymn of the day was being completed, just before the Ardas, for I felt that the proceedings after that are long drawn. I told my wife about my new found hobby.

"No. This is not a hobby. It is your love for your religion and the Wahey Guru" she said, "You should be a part of the Ardas. Only the fortunate can take part."

So the next day, I made it a point to stay on for the entire proceedings.

Actually there are two separate Ardas sessions that follow the cessation of singing of hymns, amidst beating of a huge drum, called 'Nagaada'. One is to ask for permission to bring proceedings of the day to a close and to invite the devotees to partake holy 'parshad' and 'langar' and also to apologize for the mistakes that have inadvertently crept in during the rendering of the "Katha (story telling and lessons of the past from the holy scriptures) and Kirtan (singing of holy hymns)". The other is to ask for permission from the Guru Granth Sahib (the holy book) to transfer it to it's abode for the night, "Sukh Asan" and to ask for permission to gratify the devout in the morning by it's sheer presence. (This morning ritual is worth seeing in the Darbar Sahib in Amritsar). Then the actual folding up the holy Guru Grant Sahib takes place and the head priest carries it on his head with all the devout following it amidst singing of a particular hymn called "Kirtan Suhelaji". Proceedings are as pious as they can get. One can see the devotion on the faces of the devotees. Everyone present bows low as the procession passes.

The drums (Nagaadas) have had a very vital role to play in the Sikh diaspora. When they were beaten in earnest as they headed for war, they drilled fear into the hearts and souls of the enemy. But after the days' fighting was over and langar (food) was ready to be served to the troops, then the drums signaled the troops to rally around for the langar. They also served a role even more important. That was to inform the hungry stragglers and the wounded from the enemy camps to come forth and partake what was on offer. The langar in-charge would shout at the top of their voices to beckon them. Once any enemy solder entered the langar area and sat down in a pangat (row) to eat, he was never treated as an enemy despite the fact that he had spent the whole day using his weapons against the Sikhs and probably would fight against them the next day too!

"You know, Teji, there are more than 12,000 villages in Punjab. In cities like Chandigarh, there are 20 Gurudwaras if not more. By that estimate, there must be more than 30,000 Gurudwaras in the state of Punjab. Each Gurudwara has a minimum of three ragis singing hymns from the Guru Granth Sahib. That should make it 90,000 to 100,000 ragis only in the state of Punjab. Even if there are 50 people in each Gurudwara listening to them, then the total devotees would add to 4,50,000 people listening to the ragis, twice a day. In places like Anandpur Sahib and Amritsar, it takes an hour or two just to be able to pay our respects because the number of the devotees is astronomical. Langar is served throughout the day in every Gurudwara. The President of the langar committee of the sector 8 Gurudwara, told me that this year, 15,000 people of all religions partook langar to their hearts content on Guru Nanak Dev ji's birthday (Gurpurb)! Just imagine how many Gurudwaras exist in India and abroad? And everywhere Sikhs are just duplicating rituals. How can they be bad people?"

Teji said, "I have just come back from a visit to the Golden Temple. In the kitchen, there were about 250 people who were just cutting onions. Hundreds of them were chopping vegetables. I can't tell you how many were kneading the dough and making chapattis on the machine. Don't forget the people who were making the dals (lentils), for the langar goes on 24 hours of the day, 365 days of the year! There has never been a break or a strike!"

It is fifteen minutes past 8 pm. Everyone goes their own way. This is repeated every day. I too am in a different mood as I head for home. I tell my wife, Gurminder, about my experiences. She knows me too well. After all, she has been married to me for 40 years!

I too can sense what she has in her mind. *"May he carry on following the Guru's path!"*

THOSE INTERESTED IN THE HISTORY OF COFFEE AND CHANDIGARH, READ ON

I know the question of why I should even have coffee if it is harmful for me, looms large in your brain. If one looks at the history of coffee, one will definitely pass me off as one of those millions of humans all over the world who have succumbed to this creation of God. Since the whole story begins with coffee, I thought of delving further into its' origin and it's contents that make people like me to go back again and again for more of it.

As the story goes, it all started with a gentleman called Mr. Kaldi, an Ethiopian sheppard who realized that his sheep started dancing the moment they ingested a certain type of berry. Later, the Africans mixed these beans with fat which formed edible energy balls. By then, people had begun to dry the berries and brew the powder. The rise of Islam contributed to the popularity of coffee since it proved to be an alternate to alcohol, for alcohol was banned in their religion and coffee wasn't. It was as early as 1475 that Mr Kiva Han decided to open the first coffee shop in Istanbul, known then as Constantinople. Turkey does not produce coffee on it's own though. Ghana is the largest coffee producer of the world. The coffee belt runs between the Tropic of Cancer and Tropic of Capricorn.

Teji, my friend tells me, that Turks became so obsessed with coffee that it was soon deemed perfectly legal for a lady to divorce her husband if he could not provide her with a regular supply of coffee for life! Yes Sir! The Turks take their coffee seriously. They make their coffee in small cups and they make it strong and black. And it is as pungent as it comes. To neutralize the pungent coffee, they mastered the art of making the world's best sweet meats which they devour with equal gusto.

For the want of a better past time, which soon became a habit with them, the Turks raided and overran neighboring countries with startling regularity. That time, when the itch came again, it just happened to be Austria. But as they were preparing to settle in, they received news of the death of their beloved Ataturk, which meant "father of the nation".

Atarturk (who was born Mustafa and dubbed 'Kemal' (perfect) by his fellow warriors) had a slight misunderstanding with the Sultan of Istanbul when the Sultan handed the country to the allied forces on a platter. He escaped in the middle of the night and set up a separate seat of power nearby. From there, he fought off the allied forces with a handful of ferocious warriors and took back his land. He then decided that killing the Sultan was the best way to solve the misunderstanding. Having done that, he went on to proclaim himself the first President of Turkey.

It is said that the reforms that he made in his rule, took Turkey 300 years ahead in only 10 years! The empire that the Turks created was the great Ottaman Empire.

Ah! We must come back to their Austrian sojourn. On hearing the news that Ataturk had died, the Turks, badly affected by that news, returned to Turkey, dumping everything in Austria. Even today, they address their President as their 'father'!

Catch an Indian doing that. We are good at penning songs but in our hearts, we don't respect anyone enough to mean what we say in them. But then the common man did not write those things. The poets did. Or maybe, we have set the bar too high.

Among the things that they left behind in Austria were bagfuls of their beloved coffee beans. As a consequence, a problem loomed large for the Austrians, for no one in Austria has seen coffee beans, hence they didn't know what to do with them. But soon, a gentleman who went by the name Franz Kolscitzky, sprouted like a mushroom. He had been to Turkey and had seen coffee beans there. He grinded them to powder and boiled it. Presto! Austria had a new drink.

Vienna got it's first sweetened coffee bar in 1529. U.K followed with it's own in 1652, called the 'Turks Head'. Twenty two years later, Paris too had a coffee house. George Washington, a Belgian, invented instant coffee in 1906. He created Espresso coffee by shooting pressurized water through finely ground coffee and a year later, Germany joined in. The first coffee shop of New York opened in 1972. Coffee was popularized in the U.S.A., mainly by the Starbucks Company, which ultimately opened 8000 outlets all over the world. India, despite being the 6th largest producer of coffee, supplies only 4% of the world's stock. The first Coffee House to open in India was in 1936, in Churchgate Street, Mumbai.

It was not that these coffee bars are just places which served coffee in various flavors. These coffee shops turned into places where friends and foes got together to exchange gossip and news. Sometimes, even intellectual traffic gets going. People sit for hours in these places sipping their coffee, romance, ogle or just sit and dream away. So popular were these coffee parlors, that the King of England banned them, claiming that these were places where people met to conspire against him! Weather conditions and the environment dictate how and where people sit for their cuppa. Thus, boulevards sprouted like mushrooms in Europe for the Europeans exploited the weather conditions for their tourism industry. Coffee parlors are quite a hit with movie producers the world over and these boulevards have hosted many an intriguing scene in thrillers over the years.

One glaring facility that we lack in Chandigarh is the absence of quaint boulevard coffee and food courts, so common in other parts of the world which help people to observe the world passing by. Maybe the dusty and extreme weather conditions negate the feasibility of such places. These are all excuses. The fact is that Indians are not adventurous and neither are our minds conditioned to such eating joints. We would have evacuated at the slightest hint of the water rising in Chandigarh's artificial lake, whereas people in Venice were still eating in these outdoor places wearing long rubber protective boots, till the tables and chairs went underwater. The Venetians have just reinvented life. All over Europe, it seems as if people have no homes of their own, hence they come to these places to eat and spend their leisure time.

The coffee drinkers of India, though concentrated in the south states of India initially because it is produced in the south, are now scattered all over India, thanks to the South India Coffee house. This chain has taught the entire country a thing or two about coffee and the drinking of it. The neo die-hard coffee drinkers of Chandigarh discovered a new haunt, the India Coffee House in sector 17, which is the main marketing hub of the city. Despite the fact that Malls are threatening to dislodge the shoppers from Sector 17, the attraction of these shops still reign supreme. The big showrooms have changed their interiors as well as their exteriors to attract customers, but the coffee house has done nothing of the sort.

Indian Coffee House has proved that *'it is what you have inside which counts'*.

The glitter just confirms the feeling that the cost of the product has been hiked at the expense of the buyer. The Indian Coffee House has maintained the ambience and the original taste of coffee available in all its outlets across the country. That is the only thing it has maintained. The prices have really gone up, but then that has to be overlooked for the cost of living has gone out of hand all over, so why not the Indian Coffee House. The dosas, vada, idlis and the sambar are basically what the Coffee House was famous for. The coffee was the icing on the cake.

There is an interesting story about a regular at the coffee house many years ago, who, on a cold winter morning, was so broke that he contemplated suicide. His friends advised him to sit and discuss the whole thing over a cup of strong coffee. Their argument was simple. If he has to die at all, why not try his luck in the USA first? The US of A is the accepted panacea for all ills, the world over. The idea appealed to him and he hitch hiked his way via Iran, Iraq and other countries which lay on his path to the U.S.A. This journey kept his mind off the suicide that he was contemplating. Wonder of wonders, he reached the border of Mexico and America. Since he had nothing to lose and everything to gain, he joined a gang which was in the business of smuggling perfume. Again the risky business of smuggling kept his mind busy. He took risks which only a man who has already declared himself dead can take. His destiny and providence saw him through his ventures and soon, the supposed-to-be-dead-man was a big man and became the perfume King of that country. Soon, he couldn't wait to live life larger than life itself. He developed a passion to own cars which once belonged to the rich and famous of the movie industry, sports icons and Czars of industry. At the last count, he had more than 200 limousines in his collection, which were housed in a huge hanger.

He has an enviable mansion on a hill guarded by armed guards around the perimeter of his property in the company of vicious dogs. Judges, police chiefs and senior politicians are his best friends. Money continues to cascade in torrents straight into his bank vaults.

Obviously, with a history of that kind behind coffee, I have to have at least one cup of coffee every day.

After my father's death way back in 1966, we shifted to Chandigarh for the sole reason that he owned a plot of land in this hitherto unknown city. When the great partition of India took place in 1947, my father and his family lost everything to the newly created Pakistan. The Indian government decided to dish out plots of land in specified cities to the people displaced as a result thereof, as compensation according to the losses suffered by the individual 'refugee' family as they were called. It wasn't free but what my father had to pay for it was a pittance compared with today's going rate. No one wanted to come to stay in a city which was there only on paper.

The American town planner, Albert Meyer had been chosen to lead the team for the construction of Chandigarh, the city named after Chandi, the Goddess of Power. Nowicki was second in command but he suddenly died in a plane crash shortly after. Maybe Albert Meyer took the death of Nowicki as a bad omen and abandoned the project. It was then that Charles Edourd Jeaneret, also known as Le Corbusier was chosen to complete the project along with Maxwell Fry, Jane Drew and Piere Jeaneret.

People had to be coaxed by the then Chief Minister of Punjab, Sardar Pratap Singh Kairon, to come and build their houses in this city. Slowly, Chandigarh began to take shape. As expected, the initial growth was very slow. My father was in the army so he wasn't expected to build and shift into Chandigarh. He did the next best thing. He bought the plot and promptly forgot all about it. Twenty years later, when he died, my grandfather thought about Chandigarh because of the plot. Thus, Chandigarh became a new addition to my vocabulary.

Those days, Chandigarh was a bud in the midst of nothingness as compared to a fully blossomed lotus flower, pock marked by cemented structures of today. When my mother arrived from Pune, with her brood of two and her parents, there were hardly any fully built sectors vis-à-vis, today's scenario, where it seems as if the city has run out of land. There were hardly any landmarks by which a city should be known by. In fact the very absence of anything worthwhile made Chandigarh livable and peaceful. The inhabitants of Chandigarh were quite satisfied with the artificial Sukhna Lake, the Rose Garden and the PGI.

Hotels and restaurants came up sporadically. Packaged eatables were not invented at that point of time. Soon, eateries started coming in as if there was no tomorrow. They resulted in world famous brands of coffee and ice creams cascading in avalanche proportions into the city. By this time, the younger inhabitants of this lovely city had developed a taste for the finer things of life. The Punjabis of the Northern region of India, were already famous for their ability to ingest humongous amounts of everything that tasted good, thus making sure that the ice cream and coffee parlors stay in a good financial shape.

Over time, one of the most famous brands to grace our city is Gelato Ice Cream. It is Italian. I do know that the Italians make good cars and scooters; that they are great artists, master sculptures and musicians; that they are notorious bottom pinchers prompting ladies to go running to the nearest chemist shop for balm to sooth their burning bottoms after a short trip to the market place. Also, that their cousins, the famed Sicilian mafia which has raised the bar for crime to the highest level, are a worried lot, for stiff competition from other home-grown-garden-variety-mafias stare them in the face; that sex is something which reigns supreme in their brains though the descent of it to levels below the waist might be open to debate. I also know that despite large quantities of coffee that they ingest, the entire country, including the President, goes off to sleep in the afternoon. They call it *'siesta time'*. Like a contagious disease, this trait has infiltrated neighboring countries as well.

And, because they sleep so much, nothing is ever safe in Italy.

But do they make good ice-cream? Don't ask me, for I go to the Gelato Ice Cream parlor in Chandigarh for an entirely different reason. My relationship to it is only because they also serve coffee to some people like me who want to spend an hour or two for want of something better to do. Yes, sitting and having a cup of coffee qualifies as "having nothing better to do"! The attempt to prolong the demise of 200 ml of coffee often forces repeated introspection, to bring out answers to futile questions that have haunted mankind for thousands of years.

If you look at the city that Chandigarh has evolved into, one could easily reach a hasty decision that Chandigarh has a population of single minded hogs who have very little to do except filling their tummy with whatever comes within the purvey of food. In order to cater to that need, entrepreneurs have opened so many eating joints that it is no longer funny. All through the day and night, the young and the old troop into these places which dish out goodies, throwing caution to the wind. Cholesterol? Trans Fats? Huh? What are they? They cause heart attacks? Whatever! Who cares? So we have Mexican, Spanish, Turkish, South Indian, Panjabi, Rajasthani, Chinese, Indo Chinese, Thai, Italian and American food joints. Recently, Syrian cuisines have been added. There are others that provide a concoction of all these. Each one of the eating places is always jam-packed. The 'in thing' now is home service. One no longer has to cook at home. It is so illogical to cook food at home when the couple is working. By the time they come back home, the lady has no energy left to cook.

Mr Kairon's life was cut short when a truck decided to smash his car on the highway. It could be a co-incidence, but there are too many trucks which conveniently decimate lives. India's President, Giani Zail Singh also met his end in a very similar manner, in a place not too far away from where Mr Kairon got killed.

Le Corbusier apparently believed that Indians reproduce very lethargically. So he did not give sufficient importance to wide roads. It seemed to him that Indians would always be riding bullock carts and even if they did progress, cycles and scooters would be the ultimate mode of conveyance. So he designed sectors with those thoughts in his mind. With passing time we found to our immense discomfort that those roads could not even accommodate two passing bicycles at the same time without a hint of an impending collision. To Le Corbusiers' astonishment, residents of Chandigarh rapidly became affluent and started owning two to three cars per family. The number of two wheelers became painful for the city roads. Accidental deaths start soaring but the population could not be contained. This point that Le Corbusier missed proved him to be very shortsighted indeed. The population of Chandigarh quickly rose from nonexistent to 13 lacs and is still rising.

But most importantly, we didn't have any high sounding names for our major roads and neither did we have quaint names for our streets. Every city in the world has beautiful names for their roads and streets. It seems to me that maybe Corbusier thought that French names would make his connection with the city too obvious. Or maybe the Indian architects of the city had no imagination. So they named the central road which divides the city into two, the north and south, as the Madhya Marg. Is that a name for a road or what? The one that goes to the man-made Sukhna lake becomes Sukhna Marg. The one which comes from the South becomes Dakshin Marg and so on.

Chandigarh has no roads dedicated to past stalwarts of whom we are supposed to be proud. Maybe we are not proud of any of our sons or daughters. May be we don't have any sons or daughters worth the effort. It has been divided into sectors and the numbering is superstitious. There is no sector 13. All said and done, we now have 49 of them. Since the administration has allowed high rise buildings, the view of the Shivalik hills in the backdrop has been obliterated to a large extent. Arnold Bhai should come to India to make a movie and call it 'The Obliterators', because that is what we are. We are experts in obliterating heritage buildings and historical monuments, which in other parts of the world would be preserved as if their life is dependent on those monuments. The real truth is that in India, we do not have artists of that caliber and people think that there is no money to be made from such renovations.

The very absence of coffee parlors with a view, makes a place like Gelato Ice cream parlor so vital to me and a few of my friends. It is situated at the corner of the sector 8 market block. The bakery and parlor which are owned by the same person are divided by a passageway but that doesn't stop people from buying stuff from the bakery, get it heated in the microwave oven and end up eating it in the parlor where the owner has put up three tables just for that purpose.

I have been practicing medicine in the sector 8 market, in the same block as Gelato for 32 years. After passing out of the prestigious Post Graduate Institute of Medical Sciences (PGI) in 1978, I decided to go into private practice rather than carrying on working in a hospital. I felt that you are just one of the numbers in a hospital, unless you are the boss. Recognition comes with a price tag. If you want recognition, you have to work on your own, in the open market and take responsibility for the actions that you take. There is no one you can fall back on or make someone else the fall guy. You took the decision so only you are to carry the weight of your decision on your shoulders. I am thankful to God that he gave me the good sense to make the right decisions. I say that with my fingers crossed for I feel that I still have a few more years to practice Medicine.

Gelato hasn't been around for that long though. The little boys and girls that I have treated during this time frame, have grown up. Many of them are married and according to the laws of natures, they have produced children too. I then go on to treat those children!

Such is the circle of life.

In terms of social sciences, this qualifies me an antique, doesn't it? I don't feel like one though. The building where I practiced has been sold so I moved to new premises on the main road behind the market. My ex-clinic in the market now houses a liquor shop! In India, we say "dawa-daru" which roughly means the same when taken into the context of medicine. But 'daru', when used as a separate word means alcohol. The irony of the whole thing is that I gave dawa-daru from that shop for 31 years, and now it is purely 'daru' that you can get from the same premises. Earlier I was three minutes away from Gelato. It now takes me five.

So my love affair with Gelato continues despite my displacement.

For me, there can be no other city like Chandigarh. No matter what you offer me, I am stuck here, for the rest of my life, that is.